Unsettled
Adventure

Unsettled Adventure

Jason Butler

UNSETTLED ADVENTURE

iUniverse books may be ordered through booksellers or by contacting:

iUniverse
1663 Liberty Drive
Bloomington, IN 47403
www.iuniverse.com
844-349-9409

Because of the dynamic nature of the Internet, any web addresses or links contained in this book may have changed since publication and may no longer be valid. The views expressed in this work are solely those of the author and do not necessarily reflect the views of the publisher, and the publisher hereby disclaims any responsibility for them.

Any people depicted in stock imagery provided by Getty Images are models, and such images are being used for illustrative purposes only. Certain stock imagery © Getty Images.

ISBN: 978-1-6632-1398-3 (sc)
ISBN: 978-1-6632-1399-0 (e)

Library of Congress Control Number: 2023902995

Print information available on the last page.

iUniverse rev. date: 02/17/2023

Chapter 1

It was a typical morning; there was nothing standing out as Finn went about his usual routine, scurrying here and there in search of his breakfast. Leaves and a few berries were all he could find, but it was enough. He could manage with barely anything to eat. He was more afraid of staying out too long than harvesting a lot, because the woods had many predators that would find him a tasty little chipmunk. So he was always on the lookout for his adversaries. "Unsettled adventures" is what Finn told Erin, his beloved, when he ventured out. The long, thin, well-marked chipmunk was dressed in his usual pale green ribbon shirt. Erin, a bit smaller, more freckled than Finn but bushier tailed, wore her favorite light-yellow sundress with white daisies along the bottom. Together, they were a great match.

On his way back home, Finn's thoughts drifted to their little home, a large mushroom nestled in between two downed logs, one on top of the other in a crossed pattern. The two trees had been unearthed during a harsh rainstorm, creating this perfect hidden spot in the meadow. Surrounded by wildflowers and tall grasses, the picturesque sight called to him, as if it was saying, "This is home." He found it one afternoon on one of his unsettled adventures. He explored the surroundings and found it very pleasant. The large mushroom was big enough for their needs. And the downed trees provided cover from unwanted visitors. After deciding this was where he wanted them to live, he returned to Erin and told her about his find. As they headed out to their new home, Erin hesitated and was scared. Finn stared into her soulful eyes and comforted her, reassuring her that she would love the new meadow.

They carried their belongings in their mouth pouches and little backpacks. They hurried to get to the peaceful meadow and their new home. On arrival, Finn hollowed out the stem of the mushroom. He dug into the log closer to the mushroom and connected the two. It became a cavernous space with plenty of room. The cap of the mushroom was enormous, creating an umbrella-like shelter.

Erin grinned and said, "This is amazing."

Finn's chest stuck out with excitement as she nuzzled his neck. Love, happiness, and security was what would be found here.

Chapter 2

Their new home settled, they went about exploring the meadow, taking turns venturing out on unsettled adventures. On one of Finn's outings, he met a box turtle named Emmitt. An older fellow, Emmitt was on the edge of crossing over. Graying edges of his hard shell and skin were a giveaway. He was eating when Finn came around a shrub and startled him. Cordial greetings were exchanged.

"Good day, well met," and introductions followed. Finn explained to Emmitt their recent move to the meadow and asked about the surroundings. Emmitt suggested a visit tomorrow. Finn agreed, stating that Erin would be pleased to make his acquaintance.

Finn raced home to share his news with Erin. Their exploration done for the day, they settled in for their first night in their new home. They placed their belongings neatly in their new spaces, decorating their new home. They couldn't help feeling the energies surrounding the meadow; the sounds of many new things came to their ears. Gentle breezes blew through the trees, crickets chirped, frogs croaked, birds sang, and the hum of the woods sang to them as they drifted off to sleep.

Mid-morning the next day, Erin heard a throat clearing and a "Good morning," from beyond the front door. She peeked out and returned the greeting, opening the door and introducing herself to Emmitt as she invited him in. On entering, the elder turtle noticed how neat and tidy they kept their home as he retracted his legs into his shell to relax.

He said, "What would you like to know about our little meadow?"

Finn replied, "Are there many birds of prey here or foxes, weasels, and the like?"

Emmitt nodded slowly, his rough skin creaking with the effort. "No more than in other meadows," he replied.

As Erin offered Emmitt a cup of tea, she paused, shrugged, and said, "I guess we will have to be on guard as usual."

Finn nodded in agreement.

Emmitt sipped his tea slowly and replied, "I'd be happy to show you both around the meadow. Might take us some time, because I don't move very fast," chuckling as he spoke.

They both responded, "That would be great."

Their tea finished and cleaned cups put away, they headed out.

Upon exiting their home, Finn said "Another unsettled adventure."

"What's that?" Emmitt said, not hearing so well, either.

The young chipmunk repeated himself so his new friend could hear, and they all shared a laugh.

"We'll be safe," Emmitt stated, and they were off.

Chapter 3

The old turtle set the pace. Steady, as not to feel hurried, Emmitt shared tales of the other woodland creatures. "A mouse family lives down that path; it goes towards the steam. Remember that if you are ever being chased." He explained that the mouse family was very friendly, as they moved on close to a large clearing. "This is what I call the danger zone. I tell everyone to avoid entering the clearing; it's not safe to go in there."

The clearing was a rolling hillside surrounded by thick vegetation and tall trees. The ground in the clearing was low grasses with very little plant life. A lightning strike caused a fire, which was the cause of the clearing.

Emmitt said, "This happened a few years back, maybe ten seasons ago."

Finn was sure to stay clear of this area on his outings, reassuring Erin to do the same. As the three moved on, Emmitt told of a structure not far off beyond the clearing. "I've only seen the top of the building through the treetops. Too far for this ol' turtle to travel."

Finn's ears perked up, and a curious look spread across his furry face.

Erin said, "I've seen that look before, and that's a no from me, you're not going there, Mister."

Finn nodded in agreement but thought to himself, *That would be a grand unsettled adventure.*

Emmitt said the day was running late, and they needed to be heading back home. Erin invited the turtle to stay for dinner and asked where his home was located.

Emmitt chuckled once again and said, "On my back, young lady, on my back." Thanking them for their company, he turned towards the setting sun and ambled slowly away.

Finn said after him, "Come by and visit us anytime, our new friend. Thanks for showing us around the meadow."

They turned towards home as the sun started its descent. Their return home was uneventful. They prepared dinner, nuts and berries from nearby their house. As they ate, they retraced their day. Smiling and happy, both cleaned the dirty dishes and put them away; weary from the day's unsettled adventures, they headed off to bed.

Chapter 4

Early the next morning, Finn was up enjoying his tea when Erin stirred out of bed. He offered her a cup of tea as she stretched; sharing "good mornings" with each other, their day began. They would explore some more of the meadow and gather food for later. Sharing the work together was enjoyable, laughing and smiling as they both explored their new surroundings. A typical day in their life, like so many of their days together. In the back of Finn's mind was the structure past the clearing. He wondered what it was, what it was used for, and how old it was it. So many questions. He decided to talk to Erin about his thoughts.

"Erin, I've been thinking a lot about the structure beyond the clearing," he finally blurted out after a long silence.

She turned to face him, startled at first but relaxed after seeing his expression and recognizing his inquisitive nature.

"What's rattling around your head, Finn?" she asked.

"A grand unsettled adventure," he replied. "We could set out really early tomorrow morning and camp out overnight on our way there. What do you say, Erin?"

She rubbed her face while thinking for a minute. She knew Finn would take off on his own without telling her. Then she would be left to worry for days while he was off on an adventure alone.

She asked him, "How many days and nights will we be packing for this time?"

Smiling, Finn knew she had him pegged. "Maybe two days and two nights, returning home on the third day. How does that sound?"

Erin replied, "Sounds good; maybe we can find Emmitt and let him know we will be gone for a few days. We can ask him to watch over our home while we are away."

"Good idea, my love."

They hurried back home and started to pack for their adventure.

Finn excused himself to go find Emmitt, saying, "I'll only be gone long enough to pass on our wishes to him, love," as he scurried off to locate their friend.

Finn found him around the same shrub where they first met. After he relayed their wishes to him, Emmitt agreeably consented to Finn's requests and then reminded Finn to avoid the clearing. Finn gave him a wink and a nod in reassurance that they would avoid the clearing and set off back home.

Chapter 5

Early the next morning, the two chipmunks headed out before the sun was up.

"An early start, my love," Finn said, grinning, "better than I'd hoped for."

Erin smiled in return, shouldering her little pack as they set out. They passed through the meadow, taking in all the sights and sounds and smells the early morning had to offer. Not a word was spoken as to not wake any of their neighbors as they trotted along. Erin thought of the neighbors in the meadow. Wrens and finches occupied the shrubs near their home. Friendly enough, but a bit noisy for her liking. As they passed the trail that led to the mice's homestead, Finn wondered what they were like.

Breaking the silence, he asked Erin, "I wonder if the mice would welcome us if we were just passing through?"

She shrugged and said, "Won't know unless we try."

So they turned towards the trail and sought out to make new friends. The trail was a gentle slope downhill, and they soon heard the sounds of a stream and chattering mice. They chose to move slowly as not to frighten the newly found neighbors.

Finn cleared his throat and held Erin's paw, announcing their entry into the mouse village. "Good morning to all. We are just passing through. We live in the meadow up the trail. Does anyone know of the structure beyond the clearing?"

Looking around, Erin noticed the village was shaped like a horseshoe. The little houses were so close together, they almost touched each other. Beautiful little homes, with plants and flowers in planter boxes. From out of one of the houses, a burly mouse headed towards them, smiling as he approached. He was adorned with a green vest, derby hat, and long whiskers.

"Well met, neighbors. My name is Elijah, leader of this li'l village. On an adventure, I see. Well, the only thing I know about that area of the woods is, there are strange happenings there. We witnessed bright lights and peculiar sounds when we were in search of a new place to call home and visited the house. As soon as the lights and sounds started, we made haste and never looked back."

Finn shook his outstretched hand, returned the greeting, and introduced himself and Erin. He thanked Elijah for the information, and they headed on towards the stream passing through the village. They looked back and waved as they turned around a bend in the trail.

Erin squeezed Finn's paw with nervousness. "Are you sure we should still be going to the unknown structure?"

Finn smiled. "We won't know unless we try," he said, laughing as he repeated her earlier comment.

Erin, not surprised by his response, headed on down the trail, still holding Finn's paw.

They reached the stream after a short hike. Dragonflies and other insects darted through the cattails and other reeds. A few spiderwebs in plain sight glistened in the morning dew. The stream was wide in some places and narrow in others. The rapids' churning water sounds were pleasing. Both chipmunks slowed their pace, enjoying the sights and sounds. Finn suggested they get moving if they were going to make it past the clearing before nightfall.

The sun high in the sky now, Erin said, "Must be close to lunchtime. Ready to stop and eat a little something?"

Finn nodded and found a level spot for them to stop beside the stream. Erin took her little pack off and rested it on the ground. She placed some nuts and berries on a napkin and took a drink from her canteen before handing it to Finn.

"Thanks," he said. "I am thirsty."

They both nibbled on the nuts and berries, watching the dragonflies dance amongst the reeds and listening to the stream gurgle. Finn and Erin sat and quietly took in all the sights and sounds around them.

They were always on alert for danger. Just then, a wren landed in a nearby thicket and chirped, asking, "How's your day?"

"Fine," said Erin. "And yours? Please don't be shy; come out of your hiding place and have a bite with us."

The wren jumped from branch to branch, hidden in a shrub, until she was visible. "My name is Ella," she said as she reached for a berry with her foot. Finn and Erin shared their names with Ella.

"What brings you here by the stream?" Ella asked.

Finn said, "We're on an adventure. Ever been to the structure beyond the big clearing?"

Ella chirped, "Many times, but only during the daylight. Is that where you are going?"

They both nodded.

"We are going to take our time getting there and probably camp out overnight," Erin shared. "That way, we'll have the daytime to explore the structure."

"I wouldn't spend the night there," Ella warned. "Strange things happen there at night." She thanked them for the berries and took flight, flying away.

"I wonder if we will ever see her again," Erin said as she cleaned up their lunch setting.

"She's a bird and travels quickly. You never know," Finn said. "Maybe she will come when we are at the structure to share more of our adventure."

Heading back up the trail, the two chipmunks started to feel the steepening slope. The trail led away from the stream at a slight incline. Traversing through the overgrown vegetation was tough.

"Clearly, this trail is hardly used by our woodland friends," Finn said.

Erin replied, "Clearly."

As they kept moving, they heard a rustling noise close by. Pausing briefly to listen, they identified the direction of the sound. Just around a curve in the trail, a skunk was foraging.

"Hello," Finn said; Erin stood behind him, looking over Finn's shoulder. "I'm Finn, and this is Erin. We are just passing through. How are you on this fine day?"

"My name is Declan," the skunk replied. "My day has been good. It's nice to make your acquaintance." He turned back to his grub eating, as if he couldn't care less that they were there, but then said, "Where ya heading?"

"To the structure near the clearing," Finn answered.

"Ah, I see," Declan said, not looking up as he grabbed another grub from the decaying log in front of him.

"We'll be on our way and leave you to your meal," Finn said.

Declan looked up, smiled, and said, "Safe travels," as he turned back to his meal.

Chapter 6

They traveled on uneventfully for what seemed like a long time. As the sun started its descent, waning towards the west, Erin said, "Might be time to look for a safe place to sleep for the night."

Finn started to explore off the trail, leaving Erin to wait and relax. A few paces into the woods, he found a hollow log that would be good for the one night. Erin agreed, and after entering the log, they put out their bedding, ate a little, and snuggled up next to each other before falling fast asleep.

They rested well through the night. Finn woke just before dawn and took in the dark sky. The view of the bright full moon caused him to reflect on what may come in their day. He stirred gently in his bedding and nudged Erin awake.

"Time to wake up, sweetheart," he said, wanting to get an early start.

They packed up their belongings and set out on the trail.

Soon the sun was creeping above the eastern horizon. The morning dew fell heavy on the vegetation, dripping on their fur as they passed. Shaking off the droplets from time to time, they laughed because they kept sharing the dewdrops back and forth, all the while knowing the sun would soon dry them off. They hiked on, following the densely covered trail. Mid-morning brought them to a spot with mostly tall trees.

They decided to rest and eat a little something. Around the open spaces made by the tree cover, pine needles covered the ground like a blanket.

"This will make for easier travel," Finn said.

Erin smiled, stating, "Good to be through that thick vegetation."

Sitting up on his hind haunches and scanning the horizon, Finn spotted the direction they needed to go. "Not far now, my love." He winked as he pointed, and Erin's head turned in the direction he pointed.

Off in the distance, she spied the structure.

They should be there around noon. So they brushed off the needles as they stood up. Shouldering their small packs, they started out again. This time their pace was quicker, mostly because the terrain was easier, but they were also excited to reach their destination. Finn noticed birds' songs and the low humming of insects. Erin started to sing a refreshing melody. Finn whistled alongside the melody's rhythm. Enjoying the moments they were sharing, time seemed to stand still.

Chapter 7

They reached the edge of the unplowed field, leaving the open woods behind. Finn's pace slowed to almost a stop. Passing a fence post, they paused to view the surrounding area.

Finn said, "I'll climb up this fence post and take a look around."

"Good idea," Erin replied.

He climbed up to the top of the post and looked all around the area. After he climbed back down, he said, "Looks like fencing surrounds the unplowed field. There are broken pieces of wood hanging down in places from the fence posts and some rusted farm equipment at the far end of the field. And there's a large house with lots of windows and a big porch. It's got peeling paint and unhinged shutters, and it's surrounded by tall grass and overgrown hedges. The barn at the far end of the unplowed field is the same as the house. Kind of spooky, huh?"

Erin thought about how time had had its way with this little farm. "I wonder what happened here?" she said out loud.

Finn turned his head towards her and said, "We won't know unless we go take a look around."

They scurried along the fence line until they reached an opening between the house and the field. They went down the driveway towards the house.

Tall grass separated the two stretches of pale gravel. They darted for the tall grass beyond the first stretch of gravel. Peering out, Finn took Erin's paw and pulled her forward. They leaped to the other side quickly, landing twice before finding more tall grass and overgrown plants.

"Good cover for exploring," Finn said as they made their way through the yard.

A ball peeked out from the tall, matted grass. Removing the grass covering from the ball, Finn noted the bright color underneath. The top of the ball was sun-bleached a faded pink, the bottom a brilliant red. Erin touched the ball, its surface hard. Not far off, they came across a wire loop hidden in the tall grass; they almost missed it. Scratching his head, Finn wondered what it was for; not sure, he looked at Erin.

She just shook her head and muttered, "Strange, huh?"

"Yep, let's move on," Finn said, anxious to reach the porch's protection.

Erin grabbed his paw, getting his attention, and pointed with her other paw, asking, "What do you suppose that is, honey?"

Just past the wire loop was a small roundish piece of wood resting in the grass, about eight inches long and three inches around. In the middle was smaller roundish piece of wood, about three feet long and an inch in diameter, faded colored bands on both connected pieces. Finn's puzzled look said it all to her. With a shrug of his shoulders, they were off again.

When they reached the stairs leading up to the porch, they climbed the three steps and came to a big porch with a three-foot-high railing surrounding it, connected by rounded columns. There were three wicker chairs, one larger than the other two, all with torn fabric cushions, exposing the wire springs and stuffing. Two small wicker tables on either side of the big chair completed the setting.

Erin imagined the people who lived there once, resting in the chairs after a hard day's work, sipping their lemonade. Finn climbed up one of the wicker chairs, catching her attention. "What on earth are you doing?" she asked.

"Trying to get a peek through the windows," he explained. "Don't you want to see inside?"

She caught up to him, and they reached the windowsill. Through the window, a thin curtain was visible, and through it, they could see a dusty, cobweb-covered room.

"Puzzling, isn't it, Erin?" Finn expressed.

They could see into two rooms. The closest was a dining room, and through a large doorway was a living room. Both looked as if nothing had been touched in many, many years.

Suddenly, they heard a chirping behind them, and Ella was perched on the wood railing.

"Thought I'd find you two here," she said.

"Well met, Ella," Erin said, gasping. "You startled us."

"The house has been unoccupied for many years now," Ella explained. "I haven't seen humans here in a very long time. Us birds enjoy the openness of the fields. Easier to catch our meals that way. Find anything interesting worth sharing?"

"We've only just got here, so no," Finn replied.

"I'll be off now, but I'll be close by in the woods. Hope to see you both again." And she took off, waving one of her wings as she did.

Chapter 8

"Let's go around the house and see if we can't find a way inside," Finn suggested.

"You want to go inside?" Erin replied.

"Maybe, we won't know unless we try," he said, chuckling.

So they circled the outside of the house, climbing back down the front porch stairs and turning towards the right side of the house, stopping from time to time to search an area for an entrance.

Along the first wall, they found a small window within a curved metal opening that went down about a foot and a half. Unable to reach the bottom because there would be no way out, they both stretched as much as they could to see through the little window but only saw fabric-covered items blanketed with dust and spider webs. They moved on, and a few yards away, they spotted a similar window and tried it, only to have the same results: no access.

After a minute, they maneuvered around the corner of the house and came to a stairway. They crawled up the three steps, only to be stopped by a door at the top. Using the top stair as a vantage point, they spotted the barn, and the rusty farm equipment in the field, and the rest of the backside of the house.

As they headed back down the steps, Erin said, "I'm getting tired, sweetheart. We need to start finding shelter for the night, don't you think?"

The clouds hid the sun's position, but there was still enough light left out for him to find a shelter for the night.

Finn nodded and said, "Exciting day, and it's kind of gotten away from us. Let's find a safe place for the night."

Leaving her at the bottom of the steps, Finn headed out, returning several times to give reports on what he'd found. Nothing special to report on each trip; no safe shelter.

After some discussion, they decided to stay under the front porch for the night. Lattice-covered space provided easy access for them, but also others.

"After dinner, I'll stand watch for a few hours while you sleep," Finn suggested. "And then you can stand watch while I sleep."

Erin laughed and said, "Unsettled adventure for sure, my love."

Crawling through the lattice, they both notice the damp musty smell created by the lack of light and moist barren ground. They've stayed in worse places for a night.

Chapter 9

Exploring their surroundings in more detail, Finn spotted a rusted metal vent pipe. Excited, he hustled over to it and looked in; it was too dark to see very far inside, and he wished he had some sort of light.

He called over to Erin, "Sweetheart, take a look at this."

She moved slowly over, ears perked forward, and peered into the pipe; she sniffed the air and said, "Go ahead, crawl inside, but not very far. Might serve as a good sleeping spot for us tonight."

Finn swallowed hard and crawled into the opening, sniffing the air as he moved forward. Soon the darkness surrounded him, the air musty and damp. About four feet into the pipe was a bend downward. Finn stopped and called for Erin to join him. She entered and found him looking down the pipe at the bend.

"There's enough room for us to sleep," he claimed, "and we will be protected."

After laying out their bedding, they ate the rest of the food they packed.

"Besides exploring more, we will need to find food, my love," Erin said.

Finn laughed and replied, "We must have eaten more than we thought. Before we go exploring, we'll gather stores for our trip home."

The two chipmunks could no longer see the sun outside the pipe, but they felt safe as they bedded down for the night.

Well into the night, a moaning sound startled Finn awake. The moan penetrated everything.

Erin opened her eyes wide and grabbed Finn's paw. "What's that noise?" she whispered.

"Not sure, but stay here, and I'll go peek out the opening."

Erin clutched his paw and followed him to the opening. Looking around outside the opening slowly, they both heard the deep, low moan again. Squeezing closer together from fright, they stepped out of the opening into the abundant darkness under the porch, turned towards where they had entered the lattice, and hurried through the opening.

There were lightning bugs flashing in the tall grass everywhere. This was the only light, the night sky cloud covered. The chipmunks rose up as high as they could reach and looked around in all directions.

Lowering back down, they whispered to each other, "See anything?" Grinning because of saying the same thing at the same time, they shook their heads no and headed towards the back of the house leading to the barn. As they reached the back stairs, they heard the moan again. This time, it was louder, causing them both to jump a little and directing their attention in the moan's direction. Both noticed the smoldering misty light in the direction of the low, deep moan, just behind the barn. Hoping to uncover what was making the moans and lights, they scurried away.

Chapter 10

They covered the distance from the house to the barn, about fifty yards, in just a few moments. Both their hearts were racing as they reached the barn's closest corner. Breathing hard from their sprint from the house, they paused and looked around. The moans were louder now; they moved together towards the sound, edging their way along the barn's front. They took their time reaching the corner. Finn stretched up and Erin scrunched down, and together, they poked their heads around the corner. About twenty yards away, they could see a rock formation. Above the rocks was a translucent, bluish-green vapor. The moans were coming from its direction.

Paralyzed, they stood still and tried to take in what they were seeing. The shapeless vapor swirled in a gentle way and flowed through the rock formations, as if touching them over and over. The bluish-green light glowed brighter with each passing touch. The moaning grew louder as the swirling continued.

Finn took in a big deep breath and let go of Erin's paw. At the same time, he stepped out from the barn's corner and stood in plain sight of the strange entity. Finn stood as tall as he could but stayed motionless.

"Ha-hello," he managed to squeak out.

As he did, Erin joined him. Standing tall and motionless, so close they were almost as one. The vapor's bluish-green light turned a brilliant orange yellow, blinding the chipmunks for a moment, but it was warm and inviting. The vapor slowly swayed through the rocks towards the two chipmunks, floating over them and encompassing them completely.

"Brave little creatures," the vapor said. "It's been a long time since I've had any visitors. I mean you no harm; I am Spirit."

Finn tried to ask a question but found it not necessary. It was as if Spirit was within him and could communicate without words.

He thought for a minute and then asked, "How long have you been here?"

"Since the beginning."

"The beginning of time?" Erin said.

"I guess," Spirit replied. "What brings you chipmunks to my presence this night?"

"Our friend Emmitt," Finn said.

"Oh, Emmitt, I know him." Spirit swirled. "We've been friends for a very, very long time. How is he? Is he with you?"

"No, we asked him to watch over our home in the meadow past the clearing," Erin responded,

"Can you leave this place?" Finn questioned. "Would you be able to accompany us back to the meadow?"

"Yes, I can leave this place. I am only visible during the night and can only move at that time. But I will come visit the meadow soon."

"Why are you here in this place right now?" Erin asked, growing curious. "What happened to the humans who occupied this farm?"

"These are their headstones." Swirling motion in the direction of the rock formations. "Come with me and look; I'll help you understand."

They did as they were asked, never leaving Spirit's light. The first headstone was the largest; they stood in front of its massiveness. "This is the marker for the parents of four generations that lived here and worked on this farm. Before it was their farm, it was my home."

The chipmunks witnessed visions in their mind's eye of the land before any human structures.

"These are my first memories. Time has no meaning to me. Animals, such as yourselves, would come visiting when it was their time. Occasionally, I would be drawn out across the valley, kind of like being stretched thin. My work done, I would return to this form and place. Eventually, humans were introduced to the valley. And I knew soon they would move in closer to my home, but never dreaming they would make a home right on top of it. We coexisted for four generations. The last crossed over in their sleep, and I helped them with their being placed in the ground. I assisted in all their crossing-over needs. After all, it's my life's work."

She gently caressed the chipmunks as she spoke. They became tired and soon drifted off to sleep.

Chapter 11

Daybreak found them curled up next to each other, right in front of the massive headstone.

"Did that actually happen?" Finn asked.

"It certainly was remarkable," Erin exclaimed. "Let's go gather our packs and bedding and start for home."

Finn helped her up and said, "Good plan, just wish we could stay one more night to ask more questions of Spirit."

"How would we let Emmitt know we are okay and would be home tomorrow?" she replied. "I think we need to go home."

Finn agreed and started back towards the farmhouse, but he couldn't help thinking to himself about the night events.

They reached the front porch and crawled through the lattice to retrieve their packs and bedding. Their packs were lighter now, with only their bed bundles and no food.

Erin said, "I'm hungry; what about you, love?"

Finn nodding and set the pace away from the farmhouse. "We must find something to eat and find a faster way home. Let's not go towards the stream but cut through the woods and the clearing. It will save us from almost having to run home."

Finn wanted to stay another night, but he knew Emmitt would be concerned if they weren't home by tomorrow morning. He decided just to go home the way they had come. Retracing their path home would be easier, anyway. *Safety first when dealing with an unsettled adventure,* he thought.

The two traveled back through the tall grass, passing the wire hoop, the faded red ball, and the wooden stick; they crossed the driveway, passed the fence, and reached the edge of the open woods. They looked back at the farm and its surroundings. Would they ever meet Spirit again or come back to see the farm once more?

Erin spoke first, saying, "I hope we will."

Finn, knowing they were thinking the same thing, said, "Me too."

Chapter 12

The open woods were just as they had left them the day before: sun shining through the tall pine trees, pine needles blanketing the ground. Finding some pine nuts and leaves to satisfy their hunger was easy. This time, it was Finn who was humming a tune and Erin whistling along to the melody. They were making good time through the easy terrain. After locating the overgrown trail opening, they made their way to the stream. Their pace slowed through the trail's dense growth, Finn having to hold branches for Erin to pass by.

"Wonder if we will run into Declan the skunk again," Finn said, his mouth full of pine nuts.

"Don't talk with your mouth full," Erin scolded, adding, "You never know."

After swallowing his snack, Finn apologized to Erin, who squeezed his hand, chuckled, and said, "Let's get moving."

The brush-covered trail slowed their pace, but they soon heard the churning stream and could see the dragonflies fluttering through the tall cattails and reeds. The stream visible now, the trail widened, exposing low-level rocks for the stream to trickle through. On the other side of the stream, Finn spotted a black and white tail sticking up through the foliage.

Motioning to Erin, he called out, "Hey, Declan, is that you?"

The black-and-white tail dropped out of sight, and then a black-and-white head popped into view.

Declan smiled and said, "Hello, friends." Coming closer to the stream's edge, he asked, "How was your journey?"

"Very exciting," Finn replied.

"Indeed," Erin added. "We found out what was causing the lights and loud moaning near the structure."

"Do tell," Declan responded, so Finn and Erin shared the tale of their adventure.

This time, he was captivated by their presence, not taking his eyes off from them, listening intently. When they finished, he stuttered, "W-w-w-wow, that's incredible. And hard to believe, but I'm sure it is the truth."

"We need to be heading home, friend," Finn said. "Please, if you ever come to the meadow, stop in for a visit."

Declan said, "Will do, my friends."

Erin and Finn waved bye to the skunk and started for mouse village.

Chapter 13

Around mid-day, they reached the village, busy with mice and their activities. Seeing Elijah across the horseshoe-shaped village, they both waved their paws vigorously and finally got his attention; he slowly ambled over.

"Good afternoon, my chipmunk friends," he said, stretching out his hand towards Finn.

Upon shaking his hand, Finn said, "Well met; how are you?"

"Fine, just fine; how was your trip to the farmhouse?" Elijah questioned.

"Incredible," Finn replied, looking at Erin to chime in.

"We discovered what had scared you and your villagers away," she said, grinning.

"Really? It didn't scare you both away?" the mouse responded.

"We were frightened, but we faced our fears," Finn said, puffing his chest out a little as he spoke.

Erin and Finn relayed their story but a shorter version, knowing they needed to be getting home. As they shared their story, several other mice had gathered around them, listening intently. Most had questions they wanted answered, but Elijah, recognizing that Finn and Erin were being overwhelmed, shut the questions down.

"Please, everyone, our new friends need to be on their way. But we can invite them back for another visit, when they can answer all your questions."

As the crowd dispersed, Elijah cleared a path for Finn and Erin in the direction of the trail. They walked to the village's edge, hand on Finn's shoulder, like they had been friends for years.

He bade them farewell and said, "Please come back anytime; you are like family here."

Erin shook the mouse's hand and said, "We will, soon."

Finn said, "It's nice to have good neighbors," and putting his arm around Erin, he guided her towards the trail that led home.

Not too far up the trail, they started seeing familiar sights: the shrub where Finn met Emmitt, wildflowers only found near their home, the cluster of nut trees.

"I'm excited to get home," Erin said happily.

"Me too," Finn agreed.

They rounded the bend in the meadow and saw Emmitt's closed shell out in front of their home. They scurried along faster, and when they reached Emmitt's shell, they gave a little knock. Finn knocked again, and the front started to open; Emmitt's legs gently contacted the mossy ground.

"Who's knocking on my shell?" he asked after a minute, his eyes not focused quite yet.

Both Finn and Erin said at the same time, "It's us, Emmitt; we're back."

After entering their hidden home and unpacking, they rejoined Emmitt outside. Erin carried a tray filled with three cups of tea and biscuits; she set the tray down, offering Emmitt his cup of tea and biscuit first.

He graciously accepted it and said, "Thank you; now, tell me all about your adventures."

"First off, thank you for watching over our homestead while we were gone," Finn said, touching Emmitt's outstretched front foot in thanks. "Erin, you start telling our story, and I'll add to it as we go along."

She did as he requested, starting at the beginning, sharing the details of their adventure, Finn adding bits and pieces of information. They told him about the mouse village, the stream, meeting Declan the skunk and Ella the wren, where they camped overnight, the tall pine tree forest, the farmhouse, the barn, and meeting Spirit.

When they mentioned her name, Emmitt's head raised up a little. "Hum, I haven't seen her in a long time," he said. "How is she?"

"Quite well, actually," Finn said. "She said she would come to visit us soon."

"How many times have you been in her presence, Emmitt?" Erin asked.

"A few times over my years here in the meadow. She only comes when it's someone's time. But you know that, don't you?" He winked as he said it, as if he had watched her assist someone cross over. Both chipmunks looked at each other in acknowledgment of what they had just witnessed.

Chapter 14

After finishing their story, Finn changed the subject and asked, "Anything happen here while we were gone?"

"Not really; there is nothing to report," commented Emmitt. "Basically, my days were like the rest have been: wake up, eat, slowly move to the next food source, nap, move again, occasionally talk with someone passing by, fall asleep, repeat."

"I guess that's a good thing, Emmitt," Finn said. "Well, we are exhausted from our travels and ready to settle back into our home; can we meet up again tomorrow?"

Clearing his throat, Emmitt said, "Why, of course; I'll be off then; thanks again for the tea and biscuit, and definitely for sharing your adventure with me." Rising up slowly, he turned towards a shrub he liked to eat and said, "See you mid-morning, my friends," and then slowly ambled off.

Finn and Erin gathered up the teacups and napkins, placing them on the tray. Finn carried the tray, while Erin opened the front door for him. Upon entering their house, they went to the kitchen and washed the dishes, dried them, and put them away. Feet and legs weary from their three days of travel, they found their couch and collapsed.

They didn't wake up until the next morning, both stretching and rubbing sore muscles.

"I can't believe we fell asleep on the couch," Erin said.

"Me too," Finn said, chuckling. "We should have just gone to bed."

"What time is it?" Erin asked.

Looking at the clock, Finn said, "It's 8:30. I better go out and gather us some food; Emmitt will be stopping by soon."

After a final stretch, he grabbed a small pack and set out for the meadow to forage. After loading it up with pine nuts and some berries (and eating two nuts and a berry himself), he started back home, when he heard a familiar chirp.

"Ella, is that you?" he asked.

"Yes, it's me," she replied. "Came to visit you and Erin, and your meadow home."

"I'm on my way back there now. Erin will be excited that you came to visit. Come on, follow me."

"Might be easier if I flew on ahead," she replied. "Just tell me the direction to go."

Finn pointed, and she flew off. "Look for the two crossed logs," he shouted after her.

"Quiet down there, young fellow."

Finn turned around and saw Emmitt slowly heading his way.

"Just teasing, my friend," Emmitt admitted.

Finn patted his shell and said, "Well met; let's go to the house for our visit. Erin is waiting and hopefully Ella the wren will find the logs and the house."

"Sounds good. I slept well; how about you, Finn?"

Finn told him of falling asleep on the couch and sleeping soundly but waking up stiff. "Oh, I feel you about being stiff when you wake up." Emmitt shared as they made the bend in the meadow.

Past midday now, they saw Ella perched on one of the logs, and Erin talking with her; Finn and Emmitt joined them. After introductions were made between Emmitt and Ella, the conversation led to laughs and more humor, all four joining in the fun. Emmitt shared some tales about the other woodland creatures that lived in the meadow. Everyone laughed at his humorous stories.

"This has been a fun visit," Ella said after a while, "but I need to be flying now; got to get back to my nesting area. Pleasure to meet you, Emmitt. I'm sure we will all meet again. Ta ta, Finn and Erin." And she was off.

Emmitt called after her, "Nice to meet you too."

Chapter 15

After Ella flew away, Emmitt turned his attention back to Erin and Finn, his face serious. "I had a dream last night," he said. "It was a good dream. I know my time is coming soon. My life is full of memories, mostly good. My love long since crossed over; she is waiting for me. All my relatives that have crossed are waiting. There is nothing to fear anymore; I am ready."

Both Finn and Erin were stunned. Not sure how to respond, Finn stumbled for the right words to say. Erin started to cry and said, between sobs, "We have just met you."

"There, there, Erin, that is true," Emmitt said. "However, will I really be gone? We have made great memories in our short time of knowing each other. Whenever you think of me, I will be close by. That is the way it is for all creatures. Surely after meeting Spirit, you have a better understanding of these things?"

"Some understanding," Erin said, still sobbing.

"If you recall, we shared with you that we felt our time with her was not long enough," Finn pointed out.

"Ah, yes, that's right; she must have been needed elsewhere if she left you before finishing her time with you. When she came to me, or vice versa, I came to her, she shared all these things with me that I have shared with you. I know them to be true. I've thought of my love many times after she crossed and felt her presence. If you think about it, if you have thought about anyone you've experienced crossing over and felt their presence nearby, you know it's true."

Finn nodded his head and said, "When my dad crossed, I swear I could feel him right next to me that day, but he was in bed. The following days, I thought of him often, and something would shift in the room or brush past me as I thought of him. I just thought it was a coincidence."

"Little signs," Emmitt said. "That's all we can receive. Only when we are ready does Spirit reveal herself to us."

Erin said, "I feel honored to have met her."

"Me too," Finn said. "My eyes and heart are more open."

"I feel honored that you are my friends." Emmitt choked while saying this, which caused Erin to cry again. Finn's chest expanded as he gently hugged Emmitt's shell.

"Can we be there when Spirit comes for you?" Finn asked.

"Of course," Emmitt replied. "I plan to stay closer to the crossed logs in the days to come."

"We would love that," Erin added. "I better get started on our meal preparation; three for dinner."

She went in the house grinning, leaving Finn and Emmitt outside. The sun's glow drifted down beyond the tree line, and the two friends enjoyed the view; no words were spoken.

Erin called from the open kitchen window, "Finn, can you get the chairs and table bring them outside?"

Finn took a couple of chairs and a small folding table from the far side of the mushroom, set them out, and returned to where Emmitt was watching the sun set.

"It doesn't get any better than this, my friend," Emmitt said.

Finn nodded in agreement, not speaking.

"Dinner's ready," Erin called.

Turning away from the setting sun, they moved over to the table, where the three friends shared a delicious meal and casual conversation.

Chapter 16

Nightfall brought out the fireflies, with frogs croaking, crickets chirping, and a million stars above. They had a great view of the stars through the open space created by the two downed trees that made their home. The two chipmunks lay on their backs, Emmitt between them, stretching his neck upwards to the stars. A peaceful and gentle breeze was blowing, the stars were shining, the moon's glow abundant, and then Finn heard a familiar moan.

He rolled over and rose up on his arms, ears pointing in the direction of the moan, and said, "Anyone else hear that?"

Emmitt said, "Yes, she is coming."

Erin's heart sank; she felt a lump in her throat.

"No need to fret, li'l one." Emmitt touched her paw and spoke with a steady voice. "I am ready. I have no fear."

A bluish-green light encompassed the area, swirling vapor dancing, touching them all over, changing colors to orange yellow. "Hello again, my friends. There is no need to be afraid;

I will not harm you. Emmitt, it's been a long time since we have spent any time together. I feel you are ready to make your journey." Spirit's energies sparkled. "Please say your farewells so we can begin."

Emmitt grinned, looked at his friends, and squeezed them both while saying, "Thank you." As the breath went out of him, his body relaxed, eyes closed, and head slowly settled down to rest on his front left foot; he was starting his journey.

Finn held Erin's paw and sniffled, tears welling up in his eyes, sad for a moment. Tears streamed down her face; she was sobbing, sad for a moment. Spirit's swirl grew more intense, colors changing from color to color, vapor's touch came from all directions, filling the peaceful night sky, as the stars continued to shine. Finn and Erin stood alone, outside their home in the meadow. Only the sounds of the meadow's nighttime creatures brought them back to their consciousness. Looking around, Finn noticed Emmitt's shell was no longer there.

He nudged Erin and said, "His shell is gone."

"I suppose he needed it for his journey," she replied.

"Definitely," Finn acknowledged. "Now I understand more of what happens as we cross over and what friendships and memories mean in our lives. I will hold these things closer to my heart from now on."

Erin nodded as he added, "Thinking back on our unsettled adventure and all the neighbors we encountered, now memories and new friends, we are truly blessed. Let's be sure to tell all our new friends and everyone else we meet from now on about our experiences with Emmitt and Spirit. That way, we honor their existence in our lives."

"Hear, hear," Erin said.

"I don't think I can sleep," Finn said. "Will you stay up with me, love?"

"Of course," she replied. "I don't think I can sleep, either."

They cleaned up the dinner dishes, just like the night before. But this time, they went back outside, lay out a blanket, and sat next to each other, gazing up at the stars.

Chapter 17

"I never knew exactly how old Emmitt was," Finn said. "If you had to guess, what would you say?"

"Not sure, maybe 103?" Erin said.

"Definitely over a hundred," he agreed. "Maybe over 120. I'm thinking about all the woodland creatures he must have met over his years and the memories he made with them. All that have crossed before him are there to greet him on his journey; this does my heart good."

A gentle breeze swept across them; Erin looked at Finn, squeezed his paw, and said, "He just came to say, 'I'm in a good place.'"

Knowing what she told him to be true, Finn smiled.

The rest of the night, they enjoyed the sounds, watched the stars, and rested. Morning's light found them tired and weary.

Erin stood up and said, "Let's go inside and go to bed."

"Right behind you, love," Finn said, picking up the blanket.

They went inside, curled up in their bed, and fell fast asleep. When they woke up in midafternoon, both were hungry. They ate and set out about their normal daily routine. Occasionally, they would stop, talk about their friend, laugh, cry, and feel.

We are never truly gone; we just exist in a different way.

Chapter 18

The meadow was filled with brightly colored wildflowers with soft green shrubs and underbrush flowing all around. Finn sat atop his log home, viewing his surroundings, and thought about his friend Emmitt. It was a few weeks after he crossed over, and the two chipmunks talked about him often.

"Sweetheart?" Finn called down to Erin from his vantage point.

"Yes, dear," she responded, stepping out of their house.

He jumped down from the log and said, "I was thinking about us hosting a gathering of our new friends here in the meadow. We could share with them our experience with Emmitt crossing over. Plus, it would be nice to see everyone again; what do you think?"

Erin grinned and replied, "I think that's a great idea. We will have to gather quite the harvest to feed all of them, right?"

"We sure will; I'll get started right away. We should find Ella and ask her to spread the word to our neighbors about the gathering."

"Another great idea," Erin said. "We'll be on the lookout for her flying around then."

Another unsettled adventure, Finn thought as he set out to forage for the big gathering. He strolled along through the meadow, collecting as many nuts and berries as he could and stowing them carefully in his pack, placing layers of delicious leaves between each row of nuts and berries, so as not to squish them. As he made his way back home, he saw Ella flying overhead and gave a whistle to get her attention. The little wren flew back to land on a branch near him.

"Well met, Finn," she said after landing. "How have you been?"

"Very well, thank you for asking," he replied. "We are planning a gathering in three days' time for all the new friends we made from our adventures to the farmhouse. Would you be willing to fly out and deliver an invitation to each of our friends? It would be a big help."

"Of course," Ella said. "What time should I tell them to show up?"

"Lunchtime would be great; thank you so much for helping us."

She smiled, nodded, and flew off, saying, "See you in three days at lunchtime."

"Looking forward to it," he said, starting back home and grunting as he shifted the heavy pack on his back.

Chapter 19

When he got home, Erin was waiting to help him unload his pack.

As he approached, she noticed how loaded his pack was and said, "Wow, you've been busy."

"Yes, love, and I spoke with Ella about sending our invites out to our new friends."

As Erin helped him take off his pack, she said, "Oh my, this is heavy."

"Full of delicious munchies for our gathering," he said. "I'll need to collect more in the next few days."

"Well, it's a great start, sweetheart," Erin said as she put the nuts and berries away, saving the leaves as well.

"I will look for some grubs and other insects as well as more berries and nuts on my next trip out," Finn said, "but for now, I'm hungry. Let's have a little of what I just brought home."

Erin prepared them a snack and placed it on the kitchen table, while Finn washed up from his foraging. They sat down to eat and began discussing what else they'd need for the gathering.

"We'll need some sort of long table, some more chairs, and definitely decorations," Erin said.

"What type of decorations?" Finn asked. "I think simple is best."

"Maybe some paw-picked wildflower centerpieces; that would be simple and nice."

"Agreed," Finn said. "Can you take care of those? And I'll get started on the table and extra chairs."

Their snack finished, they began gathering the items needed to complete their tasks. Finn found a large piece of bark not far from their home that was about a foot and a half long and a foot wide.

This will make a fine long table, he thought. *The only problem is, how can I get it back home? It's way too heavy for just me to carry.* He hurried home and told Erin about the piece of bark.

"That sounds perfect," she said. "Let's go."

They were both excited as they scampered off.

When they reached the large piece of bark, Erin inspected it and said, "Oh, Finn, you have done quite well."

His chest expanded as he smiled at the compliment.

"Do you think we can carry it home in one piece," he asked, "or should we break it in half?"

"Let's see if we can lift it as one piece first," Erin suggested.

They lifted it with ease and carried it on their backs, making their way back to the log home.

They rested it on the ground just alongside the log, rough side up, for Finn to attach legs and supports to the bottom so they could use the smooth side. Finn attached the legs and supports he had gathered while Erin collected lots of wildflowers from nearby their home. Finished with the table, Finn asked Erin for help flipping the table over. They turned it over with ease and looked at Finn's work.

"It looks pretty good, if I do say so myself," Finn claimed with a wide grin.

"It certainly does, my love," Erin replied.

"Your selection of wildflowers is stunning," he said. "I can't wait to see how you arrange them, my love."

"We'll need to keep them in the shade of the down crossed trees," she explained, "and water them. Will you help me move them into the shade?"

"Of course," Finn said.

They moved the wildflowers into the shade, and Erin filled her watering can and sprinkled the wildflowers with the water. "That should take care of them until I can arrange them tomorrow," she said. "Thanks for your help."

"You're welcome," he replied, "and thanks for your help with that huge table, my love. I'm exhausted; I have just enough energy to eat a little and go to bed. What about you, Erin?"

"You worked hard today," she said, "and so have I. Let's do just what you said."

The day's work done, after sharing a little snack, they gently climbed into bed and drifted off to sleep.

Chapter 20

Early the next morning, Finn and Erin enjoyed a nice breakfast of nuts and berries as they discussed their plans for the day.

"Another day in our meadow," Erin exclaims, "filled with adventures."

"Right so, love," Finn replied. "I will forage, and you will design beautiful wildflower arrangements."

"Let's get started," she said while clearing the breakfast dishes.

Finn nodded, grabbed his pack, and headed for the door.

"See ya later, my love," he called as he left the house.

After finishing the dishes and putting them away, Erin started on the wildflower centerpieces. She gathered clumps of moss to use and stuck the flower stems in them. All different types of colored wildflowers swirled in a flowing pattern, with different heights. Pleased with her work, she moved on to the next, and so on, until she finished five different centerpieces.

While finishing the last one, she realized Finn had been gone a long time.

I wonder what's keeping him, she thought to herself. *Maybe I should go out into the meadow and find him.*

Just then, she heard him call to her, "Erin, I need your help."

She scurried outside to see what was happening. Outside the door, she saw Finn pulling a makeshift stretcher with a bird lying on it. It was a small owl, probably a youngster, light brown and white in color; its eyes were closed.

"What's this, Finn?" she asked.

"A crazy unsettled adventure, for sure," he replied after he caught his breath. "He is injured; I found him near the clearing. He was awake when I found him and told me his name is Liam. I think his left wing and leg are broken. I patched him up best I could, but I couldn't leave him there because of being so close to the clearing."

"I'm afraid once he's healthy, he will eat us," Erin said with a trembling voice.

"He promised me he wouldn't, and I believe him." Finn set the stretcher down and went over to comfort his mate. "There, there, honey; it will be alright." He put his arm around her. "I did manage to find some grubs and more nuts and berries before I came across Liam. Will you help me put them away and give me a paw with getting Liam settled in for the night?"

"Yes, my love." Erin always tried to help whenever she could.

She shouldered Finn's pack, carried it inside, and unloaded the contents, finding three good-sized grubs, several berries, and a bunch of nuts. After storing the haul away, she rejoined Finn outside. He was assisting Liam, now awake, from the stretcher.

"Liam, this is Erin, my life partner; Erin, Liam the owl."

"Nice to meet you," Liam managed.

"Nice to meet you too," Erin replied, grinning as she leaned in to assist Finn helping him off the stretcher. "How did this happen to you, Liam?"

They helped him to a chair just outside their house.

"I was just taking flight out of my hiding spot in a pine tree when I was attacked by a larger bird; not exactly sure what attacked me. I fought it off but struck a tree branch in the process, injuring my leg and wing. I was dazed, but I was still able to hide from my attacker. That's where Finn found me." Liam blinked at Erin slowly. "I certainly appreciate both of your willingness to take care of me. I promised Finn, and now I promise you, I will not harm you or try to eat you." He held his right wing up as to pledge his promise to them both, his yellow piercing eyes brimming with sincerity and truthfulness.

After a moment, Erin said, "Now let's have a look at your injuries." She checked his injured left wing and leg, being gentle as she can while doing so, and found his leg broken and wing just badly bruised. "We need to splint your leg," she said, "and you will have to stay off it for a while." She turned to Finn and said, "Can you find me two same-sized sticks and some fabric? I will splint his leg and put his wing in a sling."

Finn got what she needed and then held his leg while she splinted it and gently lifted his wing as she tied the sling around Liam's neck and shoulder.

"I'll gather some bedding so you can lay down and elevate your leg and rest," Erin said as she finished tying the knot on his sling.

"Thank you both so much," Liam said. "I am tired and just need to sleep."

Finn and Erin went inside, brought the bedding back out, and placed it on the ground near their front door. They helped Liam onto the bedding and bid him good night. Closing the door behind them, they went inside, ate a little bite in their kitchen for dinner, and went off to bed.

Chapter 21

"What are we going to do about the gathering tomorrow, Finn?" Erin asked as soon as they woke up the next morning. "I mean, with an owl on our front lawn, healing from injuries. Don't you think he will scare our neighbors away?"

"I'll talk to Liam and explain what we have planned and ask him not to be a threat to our guests. First, I'll check his injuries. Not to worry, love, we will still host our gathering and share about our friends Emmitt and Spirit."

"Thank you, Finn," Erin said as she offered him his breakfast. "Remember, you still need to make a few more chairs."

"Oh, that's right," he said. "Maybe I'll just gather some small rocks and button mushrooms for our guest to sit on, instead of building chairs."

"Good idea, love," Erin said.

"I better go out and check on Liam," Finn said, "and talk to him about our plans." He headed out the door.

He found Liam lying on his back, left leg elevated, snoring loudly. "Good morning, my friend," Finn said as he approached the turtle. "How are you feeling?"

"A little startled at the moment." Liam chuckled as he rose up to see his friend. "I'm really sore this morning, Finn; thanks for checking on me. Got anything to eat?"

"Yes, I believe Erin will bring you some breakfast out real soon."

The words were barely out of his mouth when Erin appeared with a tray filled with an assortment of foods.

"Good morning, Liam," Erin said. "I wasn't sure what you would eat, so I brought out a little of everything we have." She presented the tray to him.

"Good morning, Erin, and thank you for the food." He ate all the berries and some of the leaves, but left the nuts. "Not to be picky, but I've never tried nuts before, so I'll be okay eating the berries and leaves until I'm able to fend for myself."

"Okay then, next mealtime, I'll just bring you berries and leaves."

"We are hosting a gathering at lunchtime tomorrow for our neighbors," Finn said. "They will be coming from all over the meadow to visit us. I'm hoping you will be on your best behavior while they visit."

"Of course I will, Finn and Erin. This sounds like a good time; can I help in any way?"

"Thanks for that, but with your injuries, you just need to rest," Erin said. "Finn, let's get started on the finishing touches for our guest."

"Right away, dear," Finn said, as he hurried off.

Erin returned to her household chores, humming a little tune as she cleaned.

"Erin, I don't want to be a bother," Liam called out, "but can I have something to drink?"

"Why yes, Liam. I should have offered you some tea with your breakfast," Erin replied apologetically. "I'll bring it right out."

As Erin brought the tea out, Finn showed up with a bunch of little mushroom caps and a few small stones. "These should make nice chairs, don't you think?" he asked Erin.

"Oh yes; yes, they will," she replied. "Let me give Liam his tea, and I'll help you put them around the table." After doing this, she said, "Now we are looking like we are ready for guests."

Finn said, "Let's put out your beautiful centerpieces too."

"Sure wish I could see your table display," Liam said, leaning out as far as he could to see.

"We'll help you have a look after we put the centerpieces out," Finn suggested.

They placed the centerpieces on the tables, put chairs all around, and had enough food to feed all their guest. Erin and Finn helped their new friend up to see their table setting.

"Wonderful, just wonderful," Liam said. "Your guests are going to be impressed." His smile was interrupted by a grimace of pain, and he said, "Better help me back over to the bed."

They did as he requested, easing him back down on the bedding.

"We'll move you closer to the festivities so you can enjoy in on the fun," Finn said.

"Let's enjoy this beautiful afternoon by getting to know you better, Liam," Erin suggested.

"Yes, Liam tell us about yourself," Finn chimed in.

"Okay, okay, I'm a northern saw whet owl, and I have two brothers that live nearby. Their names are Leif and Loki. We share the territories near the clearing and across the stream to past the old farmhouse. We are mostly nocturnal, but we will travel during the daylight. I hope that none of us have eaten any of your relatives ..." he trailed off, realizing that might be a possibility. The words already spoken couldn't be taken back. Liam gulped and added, "Sorry for that, but it's a possibility; I'm just being honest."

"We understand the circle of life, and we don't blame you for your part in the circle," Finn said. "After all, we play a part in the circle as well. Everything is connected in this life; no one thing exists on its own."

"Very true," Liam agreed. "I need to sleep again. I'm so used to sleeping at this time of day, and I am still hurting. My body needs the rest if I'm to heal."

"We will leave you to rest then and go on about our day," Erin said, tucking him in the bedding.

The rest of their day was spent clearing the meadow area around their home of old leaves, fallen branches, and the like. This took most of the afternoon, only stopping to eat a little and drink tea. "Let's go topside on the log and have a look at our work" Finn finally suggested.

They scampered around to the backside of their home. The two uprooted trees formed a tangle of roots perfect for climbing up or down. With little effort, they reached the top.

"This is the first time I've been up here," Erin said, looking around.

"Quite the view, huh?" Finn asked.

"Absolutely."

From their vantage point, they could see most of the meadow and all the area around their home they just finished cleaning and decorating.

"I think our friends will be pleased and excited for the gathering tomorrow," Erin said after looking around a few minutes.

"I believe that will be the case, sweetheart; we have really worked hard, and it shows," Finn replied.

The sun's fading light cast long shadows in their meadow home, and long pillars of sunlight reached down through the trees like golden streams. They stood arm in arm, taking in all that was being given to them at that moment.

"I'm thinking of Spirit and Emmitt and about the energies they gifted us," Finn said. "And how different life seems to be now."

"Yes, me too, love," Erin said.

They enjoyed the moment a little longer, slowly coming back from their meditation to their place on top of the log.

"We better go back down and feed our patient and ourselves." Erin chuckled as she said it because she didn't want the moment to end.

"Yes, we should head back down. I'm sure Liam is hungry by now."

They climbed down, prepared dinner, and shared the meal with Liam outside.

"Did you rest well?" Finn asked.

"Quite well," Liam answered. "This meadow is very beautiful and peaceful."

"That's good; we are glad you find our little meadow to your liking." Erin added, "We have a big day happening tomorrow, so we need to get a good night's rest and so do you. If you need anything during the night, just call out to us. Rest well."

She then gathered up the dinner dishes, placed them on the tray, and brought them inside. Finn bid Liam good night and followed Erin inside. They washed the dinner dishes, dried them, and put them away. After they finished, they went to bed, cuddling up next to each other and falling fast asleep.

Chapter 22

Morning's daylight greeted Liam, sleeping outside the home of his caretaker friends. Having been up off and on throughout the night, Liam slept soundly, taking advantage of the cool morning air until he was woken by Erin's gentle voice, saying, "Good morning, Liam; how are you feeling?"

"Good morning, Erin, I'm feeling stiff and sore," Liam replied.

"I've made you some willow bark tea," she said, "and I want you to chew on this piece of willow bark; both will help with your pain. Here are some biscuits too."

"Thank you; your kindness is overwhelming," Liam said while sipping on the tea and eating a biscuit.

"You are welcome," Erin replied. "Hopefully, you would do the same for others. After all, we are all related, coming from our Mother Earth."

Finn stepped through the doorway with a biscuit in his hand. "Good morning, friend, I see you are on the mend. Did you rest well?"

"Yes, I was awake off and on; nighttime is my usual time for hunting, so I would normally be awake all night, but I did rest very well."

"Glad you rested well. We better start getting ready for our guests, love," Finn told Erin. "Let's move Liam over closer to the table first."

Both chipmunks helped Liam stand and assisted him in walking over to the table. Finn gathered up the bedding and brought it to where Liam would rest during the gathering.

After settling him in again, elevating his leg, and checking his wing, Erin asked, "How's that for you?"

"Just fine, once again, thank you both so very much," Liam exclaimed. "Now don't be concerned with me; go finish getting ready for your guests. They'll be here soon."

"Okay, we are going to go do just that," Finn said.

Erin brought all the food out, making several trips, and arranged it on the big table around the wildflower centerpieces. Finn carried a tray filled with plates and cups, placing them all around the big table. When they finished, they took a moment to look at their creation. "Looks great," she said.

"Agreed," Finn said.

"We better get ourselves ready now, love."

Holding paws, they walked past Liam, resting with his eyes closed, willow bark sticking out of his beak, and headed into their house. A little later, Erin and Finn emerged from their house, ready to greet their guests.

Liam said, "Both of you look cleaned up and ready."

"Why, thank you, Liam," Erin answered.

Just then, Ella landed on the ground a few feet away and chirped, "Hello, friends, who is this?"

"I'm Liam, and you are?"

"My name is Ella. I see you're hurt; what happened?"

"Let's wait until all the guests are here, and then I can explain my being here, okay?" Liam suggested.

"Good idea," Finn said, "and let's wait to make all the introductions too. Good to see you again, Ella; were you able to find all of our friends and invite them to our party?"

"Oh yes, and they all said they are coming," she responded.

Erin and Finn smiled, and Erin clapped her paws together and said, "I can't wait."

Soon, the meadow was filled with all their friends. Elijah and his mice family were all there, about twelve in all, Declan came strolling in casually shortly after them, and Ella completed the guest list.

"Please, everyone gather around the table," Finn announced. "This is Liam." He helped the owl up and into a seated position at the table, and introductions commenced, all exchanging their names with Liam.

Everyone settled back into their seats, Liam told them all about how he came to be in the care of Finn and Erin.

When finished, Erin said, "He has been the most gracious patient and now our friend."

"Hear, hear," Finn added. "Please, everyone, help yourselves to the feast, and visit with each other. Later, we will tell you all why we asked you to come here."

Chapter 23

All their guests helped themselves to the bountiful spread laid out in front of them. Different conversations were happening all at the same time.

"Declan, I found some grubs for you," Finn said. "Please help yourself to them. How have you been getting along?"

"Very well," Declan answered while taking a bite of grub. "Things by the stream are pretty much the same as when we first met. Besides your li'l adventure with Liam, how are things with you and Erin?"

"Things have been good," Finn said. "We are enjoying our new home and exploring the meadow more and more."

"That sounds good to me, friend," Declan said, lifting his cup up to toast Finn; they clinked cups and laughed.

Erin was chatting with the mice.; Elijah introduced her to his family.

"Erin, this is my spouse, Molly," he said. "We are certainly glad to be here today."

"You have a beautiful place here in the meadow," Molly told Erin.

"We really love it here," she replied. "How do you manage with ten kids?"

"Teamwork, lots and lots of teamwork." Molly laughed, tugging on Elijah's arm.

"Yes, lots of teamwork," Elijah echoed. "We work really well together, and so do our kids."

"Most of our relatives live in our village," Molly added, "and we all pitch in helping take care of everyone."

"That's fantastic," Erin said, watching the mice children playing in the meadow.

Ella was talking to Liam.

"What kind of bird do you think attacked you?" she asked.

"I'm not sure," he said, "it all happened so fast, and before I knew it, I was on the ground under some dense foliage. I think that's what saved me from whatever it was, plus Finn coming along offering me aid. He was amazing, binding my wounds, finding pine branches long enough to make a stretcher, with plenty of pine needles to protect me while he pulled me here. He had to stop a few times, and once, I thought he would have to leave me and come get Erin to help get me all the way here, but after a long rest, he was able to pull me the rest of the way."

"He is a very special chipmunk," Ella said, "and so is Erin."

Finn stood up, took his spoon, and clinked on the side of his cup to get everyone's attention. Erin was standing next to him.

"First of all," he said, "we want to thank you all for coming here today. We invited you here to share with you our experiences with our friend Emmitt and Spirit. You all know Emmitt, and most of you have heard about our unsettled adventure to the farmhouse, where we met Spirit. When we returned home, Emmitt was waiting for us; we had asked him to watch over our home while we were gone on our adventure.

"He knew of Spirit, having met her on multiple occasions over the course of his life. The next day, after we returned home, Emmitt came back for a visit. Ella, you met him that day, and we all shared some laughs before you had to leave. He stayed with us all day and told us his time here was coming to an end. That evening, Spirit came and helped him cross over. It was a peaceful experience; he was ready and welcomed the next part of his journey. When his time came, the meadow was filled with a swirling, bright orange yellow light; Spirit's energy took him on his journey, leaving nothing behind." He reached over to hold Erin's paw, his eyes tearing up. "What we learned is that every time we think or talk about him, he is nearby; there might be the smallest of things that move or change in the space. That is him. That's the way it is for everything that crosses over. We just wanted to tell you all about our new understanding of our shared memories. We are never truly gone; we just exist in a different way. Thank you for listening."

After Finn finished, he sat back down, and Erin followed his lead.

Chapter 24

For several moments, no one spoke, and then Declan broke the silence, saying, "I wish I had known Emmitt better; we were cordial in passing, but most creatures give me a wide birth. I've never met Spirit before, but the way you both described her, she sounds magnificent."

"We spent many afternoons with Emmitt," Elijah said. "He often came to our village on his way to the stream. He told us stories of our woodland home and surrounding areas. He was more of a teacher than a storyteller, warning us of dangers, helping us find food when it was scarce, never asking for anything in return. He was a good friend. Never had the pleasure of meeting Spirit either, but as Declan said, she sounds magnificent."

"I observed Emmitt on lots of occasions," Ella chirped, "but never had the pleasure of meeting him until the day I came here to visit Finn and Erin. I wish I had stopped and introduced myself sooner as I flew overhead.

"The night that Finn described, I was hunting nearby, tucked away in one of my many hiding places. When I saw the bright light, I left my hiding spot to see what it was, afraid it might be a fire spreading. But to my surprise, it wasn't a fire but a brilliant orange yellow light covering all the open meadow. I wasn't sure what was happening, so I took flight away from the light. Now that I've been blessed to meet Erin and Finn, mystery solved."

"Seems like we all have memories of or about Emmitt and Spirit," Erin announced. "Let's not let those memories fade. This was a good thing to do today; we should get together again soon. Now, can I get some help clearing the dishes and washing them?"

Molly started stacking up the dishes near her, and Ella nudged the cutlery into a pile from around the table. Elijah and Declan carried the stacks of dishes and the cutlery into the house. Finn put the cups on a tray and followed Elijah and Declan into the house.

"Wish I could lend a wing to help, but I'm a little banged up," Liam said, chuckling.

"Thank you all for helping me," Erin said, carrying the last of the dishes into the house.

Molly offered to help Erin wash and dry the dishes, asking her two oldest daughters to help as well. They had their tasks done in no time and rejoined the rest of the gathering back outside.

"Thank you, ladies, for doing all those dishes," Finn said when they rejoined the others.

"It was our pleasure," Molly said. "After all, you and Erin did so much work getting this all put together."

Everyone seated themselves back around the table and started visiting again.

"We couldn't have asked for better weather for this today, could we?" Finn said to everyone.

"It has been perfect weather today, not too hot, and the right amount of wind," Liam agreed.

Others around the table nodded in agreement.

"This has been really fun meeting everyone and sharing a terrific meal too," Elijah announced, "but it's getting late, and by the time we travel back to the village, it will be almost dark out." He called for their kids to gather around.

"Thank you again for everything, Erin and Finn," Molly said. "We do need to be getting our crew heading home."

Saying bye to the rest of the guests, they scurried off in the direction of the village.

Soon Ella said farewell and thanked Erin and Finn, waving bye to Declan and Liam and promising, "See you all soon."

She took flight and was gone out of sight in seconds.

"Can I do anything to help you both before I head back to the stream area?" Declan asked.

"Nothing, friend," Erin replied, shaking his paw. "We are so glad you made the trip here today. I'm sure we will be visiting you soon, and please feel free to come see us anytime."

"Then I hope to see you both very soon; bye for now." He shook Finn's paw and ambled down the same trail the mice went.

"I'll be fine right here for the night," Liam suggested. "You two have already done so much today; you need to take it easy."

"Thank you, Liam," Finn said. "I think we are pretty tired; it was a good day, though. We are so happy you are here to make memories with us."

"Let's get you laid back down on the bedding and get that leg of yours elevated." Erin said, helping him get settled.

Liam groaned as Erin lifted his leg.

"Still in a lot of pain?" Finn asked, standing close by.

"Yes," Liam replied. "Sitting up for so long today, my leg is throbbing, but I'll be fine once I get settled."

"Here's some more willow bark for you to chew on," Erin said. "It will help with the pain."

"We hope you rest well," Finn added. "Good night."

"Just call out if you need anything during the night," Erin said. "Rest well."

The two chipmunks decided to go for a little walk before turning in for the night. They traversed through the meadow, past the wildflowers and the tall ferns, looping round in a big circle, noticing more mushrooms as they walked.

"I think today went very well," Erin said after pointing out the mushrooms. "It was really nice to visit with everyone. I'm so glad we had the gathering."

"Me too, love. It was a great day. Wow, I think those mushrooms form a large circle. Not sure I remember them being there before."

"Maybe it's Emmitt's way of showing us he was with us today."

"Maybe," Finn said.

They returned home in silence, pondering the day's events. Exhausted, they turned in for the night.

Chapter 25

The next few days were uneventful. Liam rested and was recovering nicely, thanks to Finn and Erin's care. He was able to move his wing but not fully yet. His leg, still splinted, was the worst of his injuries, but he was able stand on it using a crutch Finn had fashioned out of an oak branch.

"Keep moving your wing as much as you can," Erin encouraged. "Does the crutch bother your wing much?"

"It's a little uncomfortable," Liam responded, "but I'll manage. Finn, you did an amazing job making this crutch for me; you're very handy."

"Thank you," Finn said. "I'm so glad it fits and you are able to use it. Your wing will be healed soon, and you will be able to fly, but I'm afraid landing will not happen for a little while longer."

"Oh, I'm not ready to try to fly just yet. I think it will be another week before my leg is strong enough to take the splint off and maybe walk on it."

"Just take it easy, friend," Erin said. "There is no need to rush; you are welcome to stay here as long as it takes for you to heal properly."

"I really appreciate that, but I'm afraid if I'm gone too long from my territory, another owl will take it over, and I'll have to move away from my brothers. I bet they are worried about me by now. It's not unusual for us to go weeks without visiting each other, but we can hear each other's calls at night and know we are doing okay. This is the longest I've gone without hearing them and them hearing me. I'm sure they have tried to find me and possibly searched my territory. But we are so very far away from there, I cannot hear their calls or them hear my calls. The last two nights, I've called out but didn't hear any other owls. This scares me because of what happened to me. Whatever attacked me could be hunting my brothers, and they could be hurt too." Liam's yellow eyes and brows showed his concern.

"What can we do to help?" Finn asked, looking at Erin for approval.

"Yes, what can we do to help?" Erin echoed.

"I hate to ask because you've already done so much to take care of me, but could you spend a night or two in my territory and hopefully find my brothers to let them know what's happened to me?"

"Of course, I will," Finn said smiling. "I'll need to pack and get things ready. I can go this afternoon and set up camp."

"Thank you both very much. How can I ever repay you?" Liam smiled with relief.

Erin and Finn gathered the things he needed for two nights of camping.

"I have an idea," Finn said. "What if I go to the clearing, set up camp, and then come back here so we can use the stretcher and take Liam back to the clearing? That way, he can call out to his brothers, and we can meet them. How does that sound to you, love?"

Erin smiled, indicating her approval. "Let's go tell Liam our plan," she said.

They returned to where Liam was lying down and shared their plan with him.

"That's a good idea," he said. "I should have thought of it."

Finn shouldered his pack and left for the clearing, bidding Erin and Liam farewell and assuring them he would be back soon. Holding his walking stick in his paw, he set a quick pace, making the bend in the meadow and was soon out of view.

Chapter 26

By mid-day, the weather was pleasant, and Finn walked along, whistling and enjoying the sights and sounds and smells around him in the woods. Rounding a large tree, he almost ran right into a bullfrog. Startled, they both jumped, the frog leaping clear over Finn, who crouched down.

Finn turned around, still in a crouch, and saw the frog land; facing the frog, he said, "Well, hello; my name is Finn, and yours is?"

"So sorry, my name is Melody," the frog said. "You gave me such a fright."

They both laughed and smiled.

"Likewise, nice to meet you," Finn said. "Are you new to the meadow?"

"Oh no," she answered. "I live by the stream but like to come into the woods from time to time to visit my friend Emmitt. He usually visits me this time of year for a few days, and we enjoy catching up. I was expecting him to show up weeks ago, and when he didn't, I got concerned and decided to come look for him. Do you know Emmitt? Do you know where I can find him?"

"Yes, I know Emmitt. I hate to be the one to tell you, but Emmitt crossed over recently. Erin, my wife, and I were with him when his time came.

"If you are not in a hurry to get back to the stream, I'm on my way to the clearing to set up camp for myself, Erin, and our injured friend, Liam. You are more than welcome to join us, and we can tell you more of our time with Emmitt. Would you like to come along?"

"I'm in no hurry," Melody replied sadly. "I would love to join you."

"Very well then," Finn said. "I'm kind of in a hurry to get to the clearing; after I get camp set up, I need to go back to my house, get Erin and Liam, and bring them to the camp, all before nightfall."

"I can help set up camp while you go back and get your family," Melody suggested.

"That would be great, thank you. Liam is not our child, actually; he's an injured owl I found several days ago. I brought him home, and we have been taking care of him ever since."

When they got to the clearing, Finn took off his pack and rested it next to a tree; he said, "This spot will do. I'll be back soon. Be careful; Emmitt told us this was the danger zone. Thanks again for your willingness to join us on our unsettled adventure. Bye for now."

And he was off, leaving Melody to explore the area.

"See you soon," she called after him. "I'll have camp set up by the time you get back."

Finn ran all the way home, knowing the time spent meeting Melody had delayed him. He made good time, because he wasn't carrying his pack anymore. When he reached the bend in the meadow, he saw Liam and Erin, Liam already laying on the stretcher. Huffing and puffing from his run, Finn hugged Erin and shook Liam's outstretched wing.

"Well met, friend," Liam said. "Why were you running?"

"I was in a hurry," Finn explained. "I was delayed. I'll tell you on our way to the clearing what happened to me. Have you been waiting long?"

He and Erin lifted the stretcher, carrying it with ease. Erin had strapped the food stores for the two days at the top along with some bedding, leaving plenty of room for Liam to ride on the pine branches at the bottom.

"Great job getting everything ready to go, sweetheart," Finn said, excited.

"You are welcome," Erin replied. "Now tell us why you were delayed."

Chapter 27

Finn shared with Erin and Liam about meeting Melody and explained that she was friends with Emmitt and was waiting for them at the camp.

"She wants to learn more about our time with Emmitt and his last night with us," he said.

After they walked awhile, Finn said, "We are not far off now."

The edge of the clearing was thick and full of vegetation, making dragging the stretcher more difficult. They stopped a couple of times to have Liam stand up and shift the stretcher around a sharp turn and then helped him lay back down. Following the path he had taken before with Melody, Finn found the camp with ease.

"Hello, Melody; goodness, you've been busy," Finn said when he noticed the cleared-out space for their camp.

Melody had dragged all the sticks and moved the little rocks and pebbles, forming a circle around their little campsite.

"Busy indeed, I'd say," Erin said. "Thank you so much for making this space for us. I'm Erin, and this is our friend, Liam."

"Well met, Melody," Liam said. "Finn told us of your meeting and your willingness to camp with us. I certainly am grateful for all the work you've done here.

"Hello, everyone," Melody croaked. "What else can I help you with?"

"You've done enough," Finn said. "Just relax now, and after we get settled, I'll lay out dinner for everyone." He then helped Liam from the stretcher to a leaning sitting position up against the tree.

Melody took a seat next to him and asked, "Do you mind telling me about how you got hurt?"

Liam shared the story of how he was injured and about Finn rescuing him, while Erin and Finn unpacked the stretcher and laid the bedding out for all to use, making one for Melody and one for Liam; they would share a blanket.

While Finn finished with the bedding, Erin brought out the pack with the food stores, unpacking a few berries, biscuits, and nuts, and announced, "Dinner's ready."

"No need to worry about me," Melody said. "I caught my dinner just before you all showed up, a few insects."

"Thank you for telling me how you got injured," she said to Liam. "Can I bring you some food?"

"Yes, please," Liam said. "Just no nuts, thanks."

"I'm really hungry," Finn said. "How about you, sweetheart?"

"Pulling the stretcher has definitely got my appetite up," Erin answered, chewing on a walnut.

"Not to trouble you, Erin, but do you have any more of that willow bark?" Liam asked. "My leg is aching from the bouncy ride on the stretcher. By the way, thank you both for pulling me all the way here."

"Yes, I packed some for you," she said. "It's in your little pack next to you."

"It was no trouble carrying you here, Liam," Finn said. "Hopefully, you can call out during the night to your brothers, and they'll find us here."

"Let's hope that plan works," Liam said, chewing on the willow bark.

"Finn, you had mentioned earlier today about finishing your tale of Emmitt's last day before crossing over," Melody said. "Will you finish it now?"

Finn and Erin took turns telling the story of their time with Emmitt and Spirit. They shared of having all their neighbors over for a gathering just a few days ago. Liam drifted off to sleep while they were talking, but then he woke up. The daylight had changed from bright to dusk while he had slept.

"I guess I need to stay awake and make some calls, so my brothers will hear and answer," he said. He began to call, "Whoooot, hooot." Long and short calls, pausing between the calls for long moments.

Everyone sat in silence, listening intently.

Liam called again, "Whoooot, hooot."

Silence again, everyone still listening, long moments pass, longer than the ones before.

"It's still early," he said after a bit. "I'll try again later in the night. In the meantime, Melody, we've told you all about ourselves and our adventures; please tell us about yourself and any of your adventures."

Chapter 28

"There is not much to tell compared to all of your adventures," Melody started. "I mean, your stories sound so exciting, but I'll tell you about my life and what goes on down at the stream; maybe that will be to your liking?"

"Anything you'd like to share with us would be great," Erin said gently. "We just want to get to know you better."

"I make my home a little way from where the trail meets the stream. Just below the drop down that a big log crossing the stream has created. Above the log, the stream is narrow, so as the water falls over the log, the water pools there and widens the stream. Cattails and reeds are on either side of the stream, and there is a tree that leans out over the water, creating shade. It's a perfect spot for me and my spouse to raise our family. His name is Cecil; we have been together for a long time and have had lots of babies; some stay close by, and some swim downstream, and we never see them again. Cecil is back home, watching over our eggs right now. I'll need to leave tomorrow morning to get back to relieve him from guarding our eggs. But for now, I'm happy to be here, and I'm so very happy to meet all of you. I think Emmitt would be happy that we all have met too."

"Oh yes, he would be happy for us all," Erin interrupted. "How did you meet Emmitt? Sorry, please continue."

"We met one hot summer day; I was sunning myself on the bank of the stream when I heard a throat-clearing sound. I opened my eyes to Emmitt right in front of me. He says, 'This looks like a good spot to warm yourself; may I join you?' Of course, I said yes; he had a way about him that puts you at ease, and our friendship grew from there." Melody trailed off; just then, a leaf gently floated down, landing on the ground right next to her.

"Hello, Emmitt," Finn said, and they all smiled.

"Maybe we can come visit you and Cecil soon," Erin said.

"It sure would be great to have you all come to the stream and visit us," Melody replied.

"I'm going to try to call to my brothers again," Liam said. "Can we all listen for the next little while?"

"Of course, friend. Melody, thank you for telling us about your family and your home by the stream," Finn said.

"Whoooot, hooot," Liam called, same as before, long and short calls, pausing between listening. He did this pattern for a long time, well into the night. Everyone listened, with their eyes up towards the surrounding trees. There was complete darkness all around them now, normal sounds from the woods, crickets chirping, other frogs croaking, insects buzzing, other birds calling, but no owls called back.

Liam called again, this time, as loud as he could: "WHOOOOT, HOOOT."

This caused the surrounding sounds to stop, dead silence; they all listened. Several seconds later, the night sounds began again.

"I'll keep trying," Liam said. "I'm sure you all are tired and need to sleep. I won't call that loud again until closer to morning, so you can get some rest." He raised his left wing, stretching the stiffness out.

"Eight ears listening is better than just two," Finn said. "I think we can all stay up a little while longer." He looked at Erin and Melody for their agreement, and both nodded their heads yes.

The four stay up for quite a while, Liam making calls now and then, but each time, there was no response. Erin cuddled up next to Finn, wrapping themselves in their blanket; she fell asleep. Melody, still sitting next to Liam, said, "I'm not far behind her; my eyes are getting heavy, and I'm tired. Wake me up if you need anything." She closed her eyes and was soon fast asleep.

"You should sleep as well, Finn," Liam suggested. "After all, I'm usually up all night hunting."

"I think I will," Finn replied. "Wake me up if you hear from your brothers."

"Will do," Liam said. "Good night, my friends."

The rest of the night was spent calling and listening, all with no luck.

Chapter 29

Dawn approached; the first light of a new day started to show.

Liam woke his friends up, saying, "Sorry to wake you, but I'm going to make the loud call again. I didn't want to scare you."

"No worries, friend," Erin said. "Please go ahead and call as loud as you want."

She stood up and stretched.

Finn slowly stirred; he rubbed his eyes, rolled over, and pushed himself up to a sitting position.

"All good," he said. "Let loose with your call."

"I'm up, I'm up," Melody said, letting out a big croak. "I'll be right back; I need to go catch my breakfast." And she hopped off.

Liam made his loud call again: "WHOOOOT HOOOT!"

Moments later, they heard a loud call in return from far off.

"It's my brother Leif," Liam shouted, excited; he called back, this time with a different cadence: "Whoooot, whooot, hoot, whoot, hooot."

Silence followed for a few moments, and the call was repeated back.

"He's on his way here now," Liam said.

"That's fantastic," Erin said.

"Super," Finn said. "I can't wait to meet him; does he know you've been hurt?"

"No, I just told him where I was located and asked him to come to me."

Right then, Melody hopped back into the camp and said, "I heard the calls; what's happening?"

Liam explained what transpired while she was gone.

"I'll stick around to meet your brother," she said, "but then I need to leave for home."

"I understand, Melody," Liam said. "I'm so happy we got to spend this time together."

As he looked out into the woods for his brother, Erin set out food for breakfast; she stopped, smiled, and said, "This is so exciting. I hope Leif is as nice as you are, Liam."

"He is," Liam replied, "but he might be jittery from being up all night, and of course, because you all are here with me."

Finn gave Liam some biscuits and a few berries.

"Thank you," the owl said, biting into a biscuit. "Can you help me stand up?"

Finn helped his friend up.

"Thanks again," Liam said while rotating his left wing all the way around for the first time since becoming injured.

Just then, an owl landed on a branch in the tree above them. Looking down, he cooed, seeing his injured brother. Liam cooed back, letting Leif know he's okay.

"Come on down here, brother; these are my friends. They mean us no harm, and we will not harm them."

Leif dropped down from the branch to the ground next to Liam.

"You've looked better," Leif said. "What happened to you?"

"I want you to meet my friends first, before I explain what happened. This is Finn and Erin; they have been taking care of me. And this is Melody; we just met last night, but she is a very nice frog, and I like her. Everyone, this is my brother Leif."

Leif bowed, folding his outstretched wing across his waist.

"Nice to meet you all," he said. "Thank you for helping my brother." Leif gazed steadily at each new acquaintance.

Finn noticed he was the same size as Liam, and his markings were exactly the same. The only difference was Leif's eyes, which were bright green.

"Nice to meet you, Leif," Finn said. "We've heard a lot about you from Liam." He reached out with his paw to shake Leif's outstretched wing.

Erin shook his wing next, smiling as she said, "Liam has been a gracious patient and is healing up nicely."

Melody hopped over to shake Life's wing, saying, "Pleasure to meet you and your brother. I need to be hopping along back home now. Wishing you a speedy recovery, Liam; come and visit me anytime. Finn, thanks for being so kind. Erin, it's been very nice getting to know you; please, next time you two are near the stream, stop by and visit us." She turned, raised a front flipper, and waved at them before she hopped away. They all waved back.

"Now tell me what happened to you, Liam," Leif said.

Liam lay back down and began telling his brother in detail what happened to him, about how Finn rescued him and brought him to the meadow, how Erin has been nursing him back to health, about meeting everyone at the gathering, and finally, about Emmitt and Spirit. While Liam was sharing, Leif sat down next to him, listening intently.

Erin offered him some biscuits and berries, which he accepted with a nod, not wanting to interrupt his brother's storytelling.

Liam finished his tale, and Leif said, "That sounds like an amazing adventure. I'm glad you are still alive and getting better. Loki came into my territory a few nights ago and said he hadn't heard from you in a while; he was concerned. I told him I would be on the lookout for you. So I flew closer to your territory every night and finally heard you last night."

Chapter 30

While Liam was talking with his brother, Finn and Erin decided to explore around the edge of the clearing. The dense underbrush and foliage made their movement difficult. Large ferns and thick junipers covered the ground. Brilliant greens and soft browns surrounded the two chipmunks as they danced their way through the thickets.

Finally, they reached an opening, and the clearing was in full view; it was larger than the meadow. There were no trees growing in the clearing, only small shrubs peeking up in sparse groups. Close by, they could see burn marks on the ground, low ground cover, and grasses with clumps of wildflowers popping up in unison; the contrast of colors was quite beautiful. They could see all the way to the other side of the clearing, with few obstacles. The sun shining through the trees on the far side cast shadows out into the clearing.

The two chipmunks sat next to each other in silence, observing the clearing.

"Notice anything strange?" Finn asked Erin after several minutes.

"Yes," she answered. "There are no birds flying around in the meadow."

"I bet there are no rodents like us out there, either," he added.

"I wonder why that is," she said. "Remember Emmitt told us there was a fire that created the clearing?"

"Yes, I recall him telling us that, but I wonder why there aren't any small animals or birds here."

"Let's go back to the owls, pack up camp, and go home," she said. "I'm frightened."

"Good idea, love," he said. "I'm a little scared myself."

Turning back the way they came, they took their time traversing through the dense thickets. Finn would move first and find cover, look around, and then motion for Erin to follow. They repeated this pattern until they reached their little camp and the two owls.

Not to seem panicked in front of the brothers, they acted confident, slowing their pace before entering camp.

"Hi, how was your visit?" Finn asked. "Have you given any thoughts to what your plan is, Liam, now that Leif is here?"

Erin started to pack up the food and bedding as he listened to Liam's answer.

"Well, we haven't discussed that quite yet," Liam responded, "but now that you bring it up, we should cultivate a plan."

"We are open to whatever is in your best interest, Liam," Finn said, casually helping Erin strap their packs on the stretcher.

"Are you both in a hurry?" Leif asked, noticing the two chipmunks packing up their belongings.

"No, not at all," Erin answered. "We just thought now that we found one of your brothers, we would head back to our house."

"I guess that could be a plan," Leif said, "or maybe, now that I am here with Liam, I can take care of him until he is all healed." His tone was kind of snarky.

"Let's all keep a level head. I think we can find a compromise," Liam said, using the tree to help himself up to a standing position. Using his crutch, he took a step for the first time since the attack.

"Look at you, being bold," Erin said. "Just don't overdo it, mister."

"Easy does it, friend, but good for you," Finn said, stepping towards Liam just in case he was to topple or fall.

"I can see you both care greatly for my brother," Leif said. "I'm sorry for my tone earlier. I think it would be better for Liam if we all went back to the meadow and your house. I'll hunt in my territory and bring food back for Liam. I can fly to Loki's territory to tell him about Liam and bring him back to the meadow to visit. How does that sound to everyone?"

"I like that idea, brother. What about you two?" Liam looked at Erin and Finn.

"We both think that is the best plan for all concerned," Finn said.

"Please, Leif, don't fly through the clearing on any of your trips," Erin said.

"Why is that?" Leif asked.

"Because of what happened to your brother recently, and when we were just over by the clearing, we noticed there weren't any birds or small animals or rodents moving around. That seems very unusual, don't you think?"

"We just want you to be safe," Erin said. "After all, it might be too much for us to take care of two injured owls." She smiled as she said it, giving a wink as well.

"That does seem very unusual, indeed," Liam said. "We better get started back to the meadow." He started hobbling over to the stretcher and then crawled on. "Follow us, Leif."

Both chipmunks picked up the front of the stretcher and started to pull.

"This is a sight to see," Leif said, laughing as he fell in line behind his brother. "Two chipmunks pulling an owl on a stretcher. Loki will not believe me when I tell him."

It was about midday when they started back home. The skies were clear for the most part; little clouds could be seen through the tall trees, and the leaves moved in the gentle breeze, making shadows that seemed to dance. The stretcher was not as heavy on their trip home because they had eaten most the food; that made it easier for Finn and Erin to pull. Every once in a while, Leif would help them pull the stretcher up an incline or assist in moving the back end around a turn.

"We are making good time," Finn announced. "We'll be home soon."

"Good. I'm ready to be safe and sound in our meadow home," Erin said.

"They have a beautiful home," Liam told Leif, following behind him. "The meadow is amazing too. Lots different of wildflowers and mushrooms, mossy ground, soft sunlight; it's delightful." He trailed off, distracted by a swallowtail butterfly flying overhead. "Hello there," he said. "How are you this fine day?"

Fluttering in flight, the butterfly stalled in the air and then dropped down and circled around Liam and the others.

"Good afternoon, I am doing very well today. Looks like you could be doing better."

"Well, yes, I could. I'm a little banged up. My name is Liam, this is my brother Leif, and these are our friends, Erin and Finn. What's your name?"

"Wonderful to meet you all; my name is Jasmin. Where are you all going?"

"We are going to Finn and Erin's house in the meadow," Liam said. "Would you like to join us?"

"That would be lovely." She flew above them, following along. Her bright yellow wings, contrasted by the iridescent blue-black background, with three orange red blocks on each wing, kept Liam and the others entertained all the way back to the meadow.

Chapter 31

Soon the bend that opens up to the meadow was in sight. Erin and Finn, excited to be almost home, start pulling harder on the stretcher.

"Easy there, my friends," Liam said, laughing. "Don't want to knock me off of this thing. If you stop, I think I could walk the rest of the way to your house. Might do me some good."

"Okay," Finn said. "Sounds good to us." He and Erin stopped and put the stretcher down.

Leif gave Liam a wing up and handed him his crutch. "Go slow, brother," he said, steadying his brother as he took a few steps.

Using his good wing and leg for balance and the crutch under his almost-healed wing, Liam made his way slowly along the trail, which was pretty level and straight. They made it to a chair next to the big table just outside the two chipmunks' house.

"Whew, that was a lot of work," he said, "but I made it."

"Good for you," his brother said.

Erin and Finn were trailing behind them, stretcher in tow, just in case he needed to get back on. Finn smiled and said, "We knew you could do it."

Jasmin landed on the big table said, "Fantastic job. How long have you been banged up?"

Catching his breath from the effort, Liam said, "A little over a week now, maybe ten days."

"Oh my; well, you are doing real good to be up walking so soon," she said.

Liam and Jasmin continued to converse while the others unpacked the stretcher. Finn and Erin showed Leif around their property.

"This certainly is a beautiful spot," he said, "and your house is magnificent too."

"Thank you," Erin said. "We worked hard at making it a home."

Finn smiled and added, "Lots and lots of hard work."

"It certainly shows," Leif said, smiling at them.

"I better get some sleep," Leif said. "I've been up all night and need to fly to find Loki tonight plus bring back some meat for Liam." He said bye to them all and took flight up into the trees. After a few moments, there was a call: "Whoooot, hooot."

Liam said, "That is Leif; he found a place to sleep not far off." And he called back, "Whoooot, whooot, hoot. I told him good night."

"I hope he gets some rest," Erin said, joining the others by the table.

"We need to talk about what is going on in the clearing and why is there no wildlife," Finn said. "Why were you attacked? Why did Emmitt warn us about the clearing?"

"I agree," Liam said. "I sure don't want any other animals being hurt."

"I don't know what's going on," Jasmin said. "Where's the clearing?"

Liam explained how he was injured, described where the clearing was located, and told her about Emmitt and Spirit.

When he was finished, the butterfly said, "Goodness, that's very wondrous and concerning. I will let the other insects and my butterfly relatives know about the clearing as I travel through the meadow. I'll ask them to tell everyone they meet so the information will travel quickly."

"That would be great," Finn said.

"I better get started then," she said. "I have enjoyed meeting all of you and hope to see you again soon."

She flew off in the opposite direction of the clearing. Liam watched her until she was out of sight.

"She was very pretty, wasn't she?" he said, as if no one else could hear him.

However, both chipmunks heard him but didn't say anything.

"Maybe when Leif and Loki are here, we can come up with a plan to find out what is causing the mystery in the clearing," Liam said.

"Yes, we could set up a surveillance grid," Finn added.

"Maybe we can reach out to Elijah and Declan and Melody via Ella again and ask for their help too," Erin suggested.

"Great idea, sweetheart," Finn said. "Sounds like we have a plan coming together. Now we just need to put it into action."

Chapter 32

The rest of the day, the three friends relaxed; Liam napped, and Finn and Erin unloaded the stretcher and put their belongings away. After that, they ate a snack and decided to go outside and lay on a blanket so they could enjoy the meadow.

Finn explained to Erin what he was planning for the next day. "In the morning, I'll go out and look for Ella. I'll make my way towards the mouse village. If I don't see her before I reach the village, I'll visit Elijah and Molly. I'll tell them our plan and ask Elijah to go out and look for Declan and Ella. If he cannot help, I will move on to the stream and look for Ella and Declan there. If I don't find them, I'll go downstream to where Melody lives and visit her. After that, I will backtrack my way home and hopefully be home before dinner time. How does that sound to you, love?"

"It sounds well thought out," Erin said. "Let's hope Ella is flying nearby so you won't be gone all day." She rolled onto her back and looked up through the treetops to the skies above.

Finn lay next to her and said, "Another unsettled adventure, love. I truly wonder what has caused this mystery in the clearing. I know Liam said it was a bigger bird that attacked him, but I'm not so sure. If a large bird had attacked him, there would have been cuts or talon marks on him, but there weren't any.

"Don't get me wrong; he was quite hurt when I found him. But he said he didn't see what attacked him; he just thought it was a bird that brought him down. So what was it?"

"I agree with what you are saying, honey. We do need to solve this mystery. And we all need to be safe while solving it."

"Yes, we do."

Twilight was falling as they finished their conversation. The pinkish orange from the setting sun was visible through the opening above their home, giving way to faint stars beginning to shine as the sky turned darker.

"Just gorgeous, simply gorgeous," Liam said, startling Erin and Finn, not aware he had woken up and joined them. "Not to be eavesdropping, but I heard your conversation and totally agree with you both. I am not sure what attacked me. I just know it was bigger than me, and it happened very fast."

"Not to worry, friend," Erin said. "I hope we didn't wake you."

"Oh no, you didn't wake me," he replied.

"I hope your nap was good," she said. "Can I offer you some of our snack?"

"Yes, please; I'm hungry."

Erin handed him a napkin with a biscuit and berries wrapped in it.

He said, "Thank you, this will hold me over until the morning. I'm going to go lay back down and rest, and hopefully sleep a little more. My schedule is all confused right now. I need to get back on track, sleep during the day and awake at night. Maybe tomorrow I can start to change back. Finn, you'll be on your adventure, and Erin will be here with me, so I can just sleep all day."

"Sounds like a good idea to me," Finn said. "That way, when Leif brings Loki here, you will be able to stay awake with them."

"I'm not sure if we should say good night or hope you stay awake all night," Erin said as she gathered up their blanket and leftover snacks.

Finn laughed and said, "Me too, so good night, and we hope you stay awake all night."

They all laughed hard. The chipmunks went inside, and Liam hobbled back over to his bedding and crawled in; he sat up for a while, thinking to himself, *I'm very blessed to have such good friends as Finn and Erin.*

Once inside, Finn organized his pack for his trip the following day, and Erin helped him by bringing him the food he would need. His pack all ready, they went off to bed.

Chapter 33

Early the next morning, before the sun rose, Finn woke up and got ready to leave.

After giving Erin a big hug and a kiss, he said, "I'll be back as soon as I can."

Erin held him close and said, "Be smart, be safe, come home soon."

Holding paws, they walked to the door, where they paused for another kiss; Finn opened the door and headed out for his unsettled adventure.

When he got outside, Liam greeted him, "Good morning, my friend. I hope you are well rested and ready for a long day of travel."

Finn smiled and said, "Good morning, Liam. Yes, I slept well, and I am ready to go round up our friends. I'll be back as soon as I can. Did you stay up all night?"

Liam said, "No, but I was up most of the night, only sleeping off and on. Good luck today; I hope your travels are safe."

"Thank you," Finn said. "I'll be off now."

He shouldered his pack and started walking towards the bend in the meadow that led to the trail to the mouse village. The meadow's ground was sparkly; droplets of dew hung from the wildflowers, and the morning's sunshine made prisms of color from the droplets. Finn casually walked along, enjoying the colors reflecting against the wildflowers. He started to hum a gentle melody as he strolled. Soon, he reached the trail head that led to the mouse village; still no sign of Ella. The sun's rays warmed Finn's body from the early morning's chill. He stopped at the trail opening and looked all around for Ella; not seeing her anywhere, he headed down the trail. He kept his eyes on the forest surrounding him, scanning the shrubs, and decided to call out for her.

"Ella," he shouted. "Ella, are you here?" He slowed his pace and listened, eyes up towards the trees.

He picked up his pace and soon reached the mouse village. Upon entering the village, he saw Molly and waved at her. As he approached, Molly put down the little basket of seeds she was carrying and waved back.

"Elijah, Finn is here," she called into their house.

Elijah stepped out of the doorway and said, "Well met, Finn; what brings you here today?"

Finn walked up to them and reached out to shake their paws. "Good morning, friends. I hope you are doing well."

"We are," Elijah replied. "It's good to see you again; wasn't expecting to see you so soon, though. What brings you here?"

Finn explained what transpired over the last few days and described their plan to solve the mystery of the clearing. After explaining this, he asked, "Have either of you seen Ella since the gathering? I was hoping you could tell me where to look for her. You know, she can spread the word faster than me hiking everywhere through the forest to find our friends and ask for their help."

"I saw her just yesterday on the way to the stream," Molly said. "We conversed for just a few minutes and then she flew off."

"We might want to start there," Elijah suggested, "and if we don't find her there, we can split up. You can go find your friend Melody, and I'll look for Declan. We can meet back up where the trail meets the stream. What do you think, Finn?"

"I think that's a great plan," Finn said, winking and chuckling as he spoke.

After bidding Molly farewell and thanking her for the information, Finn helped Elijah with his pack, and soon the two were on the trail to the stream. They called Ella's name over and over as they hiked along, keeping their eyes on their surroundings. It didn't take them long to reach the stream.

Finn said, "Last time Erin and I came through here, we found Declan across the stream, so maybe you could look for him over there."

"Okay," Elijah said, "but I'm going to start heading up this trail for a bit, then backtrack and go across the stream."

Finn replied, "Sounds good; if you find Declan, bring him back here and wait, or I can meet you both back at your village."

"Let's plan on meeting back at my village, okay?"

"Okay, the village it is, then."

They shook hands and departed, each going their separate ways. Finn headed downstream, cattails and reeds on either bank; dragonflies and other insects danced among the reeds and cattails, and big shade trees dotted the banks. Midday now, the sun was high above him as he walked alongside the stream; he decided to stop and have a snack. He found a large flat rock next to the stream and sat down on it, hanging his back paws over the edge, where they almost touched the water. The sun felt good on his furry face.

After resting a bit, he called out Ella's name and sat quietly to listen. He started back downstream; he walked for a bit and called her name again. He stopped and listened; nothing, so he moved on.

He eventually came to the downed tree that crossed the stream. On either side of the stream, large and small rocks were clustered before the large fallen tree, causing the stream to narrow. Finn climbed out on the tree to where the water poured over the tree, creating a small waterfall that ended in pool of water below.

He looked around at the beautiful little nook in the forest and thought to himself, *Melody didn't tell us how amazing her home is.*

As he gazed at the large pool of water in front of him, the gentle flow of the waterfall was peaceful to hear; reeds and cattails of all sizes bordered the water, insects and dragonflies buzzing all around. As he looked to his left, tall trees stood behind the reeds and cattails like guardians, and to his right were several rocky outcrops, one was large like a cliff face, dropping straight down into the pool.

Finn sat quietly for several moments, enjoying the sights and sounds and smells.

Simply breathtaking, he thought to himself.

His thoughts were interrupted by a familiar voice, saying, "Finn, is that you?"

It was Melody; she was off to his right, sunning herself on another log that was half-in and half-out of the water. She jumped into the water and swam over to Finn.

"I see you found my little hidden paradise," she said once she got closer.

"Yes, Melody, I did," Finn exclaimed. "It's breathtaking, just beautifully breathtaking."

"What brings you here?" Melody asked. "Is Erin with you?"

"No," he explained, "Erin is at home, caretaking Liam. We need your help; can we move over there and talk?" He pointed towards a quiet spot, away from the running waters.

The two separately make their way over a few paces from the water's edge, and Finn begins to tell her all about why they need her help, all about the plan, and asks for her help.

"We really could use your help; it would only be for a few days maybe a week. Would you be willing to assist us in solving this mystery?"

"Let me talk to Cecil about it," she replied. "I'll see if he is good with guarding our eggs by himself for that long. Can you wait here for me? I'll only be a minute."

"Of course." Finn smiled, hopeful Cecil would agree so she could join their quest.

Melody hopped back into the water and disappeared. Finn looked around at his surroundings and walked back out onto the big log. Resting, he let his mind wander; a gentle breeze came across him, and the sounds of the little waterfall, the buzzing of the insects, and the sun's warmth on his fur lulled him into a meditative state. Soon, he was brought back by a croaking sound; Melody was on the path off to his right.

"Ready to go, friend?" she asked. "Cecil said it was fine."

"Yes, we will be heading to the mouse village; have you been there before?"

"No, but I'm excited for our journey and to help in any way I can," the frog croaked. "Let's get started."

And they were off, heading back upstream to continue their unsettled adventure.

Meanwhile, Elijah had trekked his way up the trail's rough terrain; it was tough going, and he stopped from time to time and called out his friends' names. He heard nothing the first few times he stopped, but on the fourth time, he heard, "Why are you shouting for me?" It was Declan, poking his head through the dense underbrush.

"Finn sent me to find you and Ella," he explained. "We need your help in solving a mystery. Have you seen Ella?"

"Okay, okay, you caught me on a visit with friends; follow me. I want you to meet my friend Asher and his wife, Abby."

Elijah stepped through the shrub and followed Declan through the dense undergrowth to a small opening, where two porcupines are waiting. Declan pointed to Elijah and told Asher and Abby, "This is my friend Elijah, leader of the mouse village. You two might have passed by the village on your travels."

"Nice to meet you both," Elijah said.

"Nice to meet you too," Asher said. "We heard you shouting, and it kind of got us nervous. Is everything okay?"

"Yes, everything is okay. I was looking for Declan and our friend Ella, the wren. I'm sorry if my calling to them made you nervous."

He then explained to them why he was looking for them and told them about the plan and why they needed the help.

"Can we count on you, Declan?" Elijah asked. "Could you accompany me back to the village?"

"Absolutely, friend," Declan said. "What about you two?" he asked his other friends. "Want join in on an adventure?"

The porcupines look at each other, shrugged their shoulders, and said, "Why not? We don't have any other plans."

They all laughed.

"Well then, let's get started," Declan said, turning back through the dense underbrush before the others could reply.

Elijah let the two porcupines go in front of himself, bringing up the rear and keeping plenty of distance from the prickly quills parading in front of him.

He called out for Ella again and again, with no answer; he then asked Declan when he had last seen her.

"Not since the gathering," Declan replied, "but that's not too unusual. She might be at her nest; she probably laid her eggs and is tending to them now."

"Oh, I didn't know she was trying for a family, but good for her," Elijah said.

The four were soon back on the densely covered trail that led to the stream.

"We might run into Finn on our way to my village," Elijah explained. "He was going downstream to meet up with his friend Melody, a bullfrog. Do any of you know her?"

The skunk and two porcupines shook their heads no and kept on walking towards the stream. They trekked along the overgrown trail and eventually reached the stream, pausing for a few moments, hoping to spot Finn and Melody downstream.

"Finn and I decided to meet back at the village before we went our separate ways," Elijah announced. "So I think we should go there now. Finn is either there already or will be there soon."

Without another word, they headed up the trail to the village.

Chapter 34

Elijah and his three friends entered the village and were immediately surrounded by Elijah's family.

Molly walked up and said, "Well, who do we have here? Declan, good to see you again. Where is Finn?"

"Whoa, whoa, slow down," Elijah said good-naturedly. "Give us a minute to get settled." He hugged Molly and added, "Finn went to find Melody; we split up by the stream, so I expect him anytime now."

"This is Abby and Asher, my friends," Declan told Molly.

"Well met, friends." Molly extended her paw and shook their paws.

"Nice to meet you too," Abby said. "You have a large family. We only have two little ones."

"That's nice," Molly replied. "Yes, we do have a big crew. Would you all like something to drink? Come to the house and make yourselves comfortable."

They all headed over to their house and found seats outside; Molly and Elijah went inside and returned with a tray with a pitcher of tea and cups for everyone. Molly set the tray down on a little table and began pouring the tea, handing the cups out one by one.

Just then, they heard from a distance, "Hello, friends." It was Finn, walking up the trail, with Melody hopping behind him.

Elijah stood up and went over to them, saying, "Hello, friend; were you able to contact Ella? Hi, you must be Melody."

"Yes, I'm Melody," she said. "It's nice to meet you.

"No, I didn't find Ella," Finn said as he shook Elijah's paw, "but I see you found Declan and two others."

"Yes, I found him just off the trail, visiting with Asher and Abby; I thought it would be good to ask them to come along as well."

They all walked together to where the others were seated. Molly offered them a cup of tea and a place to sit down. Everyone was introduced, and the conversation soon turned back to the meadow.

It was midafternoon now, and Finn wanted to be home before dark. "I'm very happy you all are willing to help," he said. "And I'm sure Liam and Erin will be as well, which reminds me, I told Erin that I'd try to be home before dark, so if we get started soon, we can make it."

He stood up and shouldered his pack. He thanked Molly for her hospitality and said farewell. The others followed suit and followed Finn out of the village.

Elijah hugged Molly and his kids and said goodbye to them all.

"I'll be gone a few days," he said, "maybe a week at the most. Be good for your mother." He then hurried after the group, already at the edge of the village.

They all walked at a comfortable pace, Finn in the lead, Melody and Elijah right behind him, followed by Declan and Asher and Abby. The two porcupines, with their shorter legs, were not as fast as the others. Their sharp quills, however, offered protection from their would-be attackers. Not knowing exactly where they are going, they struggled to keep up.

"Hey, Declan, can we slow down?" Asher asked. "Do you know where Finn lives?"

"Yes, we can slow down, and I can get us to Finn's house," Declan replied, then he called ahead to the others, "You guys go on ahead, and we'll catch up as soon as we can."

"We can slow down, if you want," Finn said, turning around while still walking.

"No need," Declan replied. "We'll meet you at your house; we know you need to get home as soon as you can."

"Thanks for understanding," Finn said. "See you at the house."

Finn, Melody, and Elijah kept their pace, and it wasn't long until they reached the bend that opens up to the meadow.

The sun started its descent but was still visible in the western sky as they turned towards the meadow. Declan, Abby, and Asher had slowed their pace and watched the other three move down the trail ahead of them.

When they were out of sight, Declan said, "This is a better pace, and we will only be a few moments behind them."

"Yes, this pace is much better," Abby said. "Thank you."

"Their home isn't that much farther," Declan explained. "I'm sure Erin will have everything ready for us."

Chapter 35

After Finn set out on his unsettled adventure, Erin went about her usual daily routine. After cleaning inside the house, she went outside to check on Liam, finding him fast asleep. She decided to let him rest and go foraging for food, making several trips out into the meadow and bringing back nuts, berries, and leaves. As she traversed the meadow, she thought, *I'm not sure how many friends will be returning with Finn, so I better collect a little more, just in case.* Each time she returned home, she placed the food stores on the big table. Looking at the mound of food, she said out loud to herself, "That will be plenty for our friends."

It was midday now; her food gathering took up most of the morning, so she helped herself to a few berries and then walked back towards where Liam was sleeping and found him awake, standing up, and stretching his left wing.

"Your wing's movement has improved greatly," she said. "Are you hungry?"

"Oh yes, I could eat a little. And I think I need to flap my wings and lift off the ground a bit and land. Will you stand there while I do that?"

"Yes, but not too far off the ground," Erin cautioned. "We don't want that leg of yours to get injured again."

She watched as he dropped his crutch and began to flap both his wings, slowly at first. He crouched slightly on his right leg while sticking his left leg, still in the splint, straight out in front of himself; wings flapping faster, he sprang upward on his right leg and took flight. He only lifted off the ground about a foot and landed gently back down on his right leg.

"Not bad, not bad if I do say so myself," Liam exclaimed.

"Fantastic," Erin said. "I'm so glad the you are able to fly again. When everyone gets back here, they all will be so excited for you too."

"I'm sure they will," Liam said with confidence. "Could you help take off my splint? Just to see if my leg is healing properly."

"Okay, it has been more than a week's time since Finn found you, so I think it will be okay to remove the splint." Erin began to unwrap the bindings of his splint.

Liam balanced on his right leg as Erin worked; he said, "I might need my crutch; will you hand it to me?"

She reached over and handed him the crutch, saying, "There you go." She continued to unwrap the bindings and pulled away the two splint sticks. "Take it easy," she warned. "Don't put too much weight on it or move your leg too much."

Leaning on his crutch, Liam moved his left leg, bending it at the knee and then rotating his ankle, clockwise and then counterclockwise.

"Is there much pain?" Erin asked, looking concerned.

"Not much," he said. "Not much at all, but the test will be me putting weight on it, so here we go."

He put his left leg down and gently put weight on it, increasing the pressure downward, finding he could put almost all his weight on it; using his wing, he extended the crutch away from himself, now standing on both legs but favoring his right leg, took a brave step forward with his left, crutch at the ready, weight shifting to his left leg, a slight hobble, more from not wanting to put all his weight on this leg than from pain. He stepped forward with his right, walked a few more paces, and then returned, the crutch under his left wing.

"That's enough for now," he said when he reached the table. "I'll try again later."

"That was really good, Liam," Erin said. "I think we can leave the splint off, that is if you use the crutch for a while longer." She walked over to join him at the table and slid some berries in front of him. "Let me go inside and get you some biscuits."

"Thank you," he said. "That would be very kind of you. I'm very happy I could take a few steps."

Erin went inside and brought back out two biscuits and handed them to Liam. "There you go, just remember not to overdo it. I'm happy for you as well. Won't be long until Finn and the others will be here. You might want to rest some more before they all get here. That way, you will be strong enough to show them you can take a few steps and fly now. How does that sound to you?"

"I think you're right," he said. "I'll go lay back down for a bit and leave you to your chores. Thank you again for helping me." Liam smiled, shook Erin's paw, and hobbled his way back to the bedding.

Erin continued with her chores and waited for her Finn to come back home.

Chapter 36

Finn and his two companions made their way past the bend that leads to the meadow; where it opens up, he could almost see the two crossed downed trees, and he called out for Erin.

Melody saw the open space and said, "This is a beautiful meadow, a fantastic place to call home."

"Why, thank you," Finn replied. "We really like it. We haven't been here long, but we have found it's perfect for our needs." When he finally saw his home, he smiled.

"There is home," he said, pointing so Melody could see their destination. They could see Liam laying down near the front door, the big table, full of food, just past the edge of the mushroom cap roof overhang, and all the wildflowers that surrounded their home.

"It's pretty, like a picture, Finn," Melody croaked.

They soon entered the open spot just outside the front of the house. Finn called out to Liam as he got closer.

"Sorry to wake you, friend, but there will be a few more of us coming through here in a moment or two."

Erin, hearing Finn's voice, rushed outside and hugged him, saying, "You are home and well before dark. Hi, Elijah, Melody; how are you two doing?"

"Very well, thanks for asking," Elijah said.

"I am well," Melody said. "You have a beautiful home here, and the meadow is adorable too."

"Glad you both are well. Thank you, Melody; we really like it here." Erin's smile showed her happiness.

"Declan and his friends, Abby and Asher, will be coming along here shortly," Finn told Erin and Liam; when Finn noticed Liam's splint was off, he asked why, and Liam shared with them all about what happened earlier.

"That's very exciting, Liam," Finn said. "I bet your brothers will be thrilled to see you doing better. I would like to wash up after my travels, and I'm sure our friends will need to do the same. I'll bring the pitcher of water and basin out after I'm done. Love, can you gather some towels for our friends?" Finn asked Erin while they walked into their house.

By the time Finn and Erin came back outside, the rest of their friends had arrived and were visiting with each other.

"Did everyone introduce themselves to each other?" Finn asked, setting down the pitcher and the basin on the big table.

Erin followed him and placed the towels down next to the basin; she said, "Please, everyone help yourselves to some food and if you want to wash up from your travels."

Finn served himself some food and motioned for the others to join in. He introduced Abby and Asher to Erin and told her about not finding Ella.

"Declan says she might be on her nest, having laid her eggs," Finn shared with Erin, sitting next to him now.

Everyone else had washed up and was enjoying their meals, along with casual conversations.

Elijah said, "This is just like the gathering we all shared about a week ago, just more friends, huh?"

"Yes," Finn agreed; he stood up and said, "Can I have everyone's attention? First off, I'd like to thank you all for agreeing to help us. That must mean you all are just as concerned about what is happening in the clearing as we are and want to solve a mystery. I thought about waiting for Liam's brothers to get here to discuss the plan for tomorrow, but I know we are all tired from our journey today. Hopefully, Liam can relay our plan to his brothers when they make it here."

Finn went on to describe the plan to his friends. "Basically, we are going to set up around-the-clock surveillance around the perimeter of the clearing. After a day or two, we will all gather at a designated spot by the clearing and share our findings. Is everyone okay with this plan or have anything to add?"

Liam said, "I can pass on our plan to my brothers. I think it would be good if my brothers and I were placed in a triangle pattern across from each other up in the trees; we'll take the night shifts. What do you all think?"

"Could you and your brothers ask other birds to help us?" Elijah asked.

"We can try," Liam replied.

"If there aren't any other questions or comments, we can all get some much-needed rest," Finn said.

They all liked the plan and thanked Finn and Erin for their hospitality. Soon, they all were spread out around the chipmunks' home, finding their own little camps to sleep for the night.

"Night, everyone," Erin said as she walked inside. "If you need anything during the night, please feel free to knock on our door."

"What she said," Finn added, laughing as he followed Erin inside.

Chapter 37

It was dusk now in the meadow, and the friends had made up their own separate sleeping areas. Good nights were shared between them all, and they all tucked in for a good night's sleep, except Liam.

He decided to stay up and see if his brothers would make their way to the meadow on this night. Not wanting to disturb his friends while they slept, he flew off towards his territory. His wing healed, he enjoyed flying again, gliding through the tall trees, eyes scanning the ground and surroundings rapidly. He found a good-size tree far away from Finn and Erin's home and close to the clearing, near where they camped nights before. Moving carefully, he landed on a low branch. Using his right leg to hold most of his weight and his left to balance his landing, it only hurt a little bit.

Now perched on the branch, he called to his brothers and then scanned the horizon; he called again and again throughout the night. It had been a while since he had hunted and ate meat, so he thought about trying to hunt. Not wanting to upset any of his new friends by eating any of their relatives, he would hunt away from the direction of their homes from now on. Worried that his left leg wasn't strong enough to claw and hold any prey that he might find, he decided not to hunt on this night.

Resting and calling repeatedly, Liam heard no calls back throughout the night. As the hours went by, he looked up at the stars and moon. The stars covered the dark sky like a blue-black blanket with a million holes punched in it. A quarter moon was visible, helping with the darkness. A little breeze blew, causing the trees to sway and make creaking noises all around the woods.

If one wasn't used to being awake at night, like Liam was, the creaking sound would be spooky, but he was familiar with the sounds of the night. It would be daylight soon, and he wondered where his brothers might be. He decided to fly around the border of the clearing but well back from its edge, hoping to hear them. He flew towards the top of the clearing and landed in a small tree with large leaves, thinking to himself, *This will be good cover.*

He called to his brothers, "Whoooot, whooot, hoot," listened for long moments, and called again, "Whooot, whooot, hoot." Not hearing any calls back, Liam took flight again, following the curve of the clearing in a eastward direction. This time, he landed in a tall pine tree far back from the edge of the clearing; he called to his brothers, same call as before, and listened, with the same results. This pattern continued until he made a complete circle around the clearing, unfortunately never hearing his brothers call back.

The sun was starting to creep above the eastern horizon; his night adventures done, he winged his way back to Finn and Erin's, where he found his friends still sleeping and both his brothers waiting for him.

Chapter 38

Loki and Leif were perched on top of the root circles formed by the two crossed downed trees that made up Erin and Finn's home, waiting, when Liam came flying back into meadow. Loki spotted him first, his red eyes focused on Liam flying; he looked surprised. Leif noticed his expression change, and then Loki turned his head to witness Liam in flight. Liam landed next to Loki without a sound and nodded his head towards both of them, encouraging them to follow him away from his sleeping friends. The three owls quickly and quietly took flight; Liam led them to a nearby tree.

Up in its canopy, they begin their conversation:
"Brother, I cannot believe you are flying and using your leg already," Loki said. "The way Leif had described your injuries to me, I figured you'd still be bandaged up and lying down on the bedding."
Liam shared with them what transpired during the day with Erin's help and about this night's adventure. "I'm so

happy you are both here with me," he said; while standing in the middle, he stretched his wings out around both of them.

"We are happy to be here as well but mostly happy because you are healed," Leif said. "We have a surprise for you; wait here, and I'll be right back."

Without waiting for a response, he flew off in the direction of the bend in the meadow and returned with two voles in his talons.

Leif dropped the voles in front of Liam and said, "Dig in; we knew you would be hungry for meat."

Liam thanked them for the meal and enjoyed eating the gifts.

The sun up now, the three owls felt the warmth and decided to fly back over to Finn and Erin's to see if the others were awake yet. Landing on the root circles, like they did before, they could see their friends all gathered around the big table, having breakfast.

Finn looked up and said, "Well met; come on down and join us. Are you owls hungry?"

They dropped down and joined the rest of their friends. Liam introduced his brothers to those who hadn't met them yet and told Finn they had already eaten.

"I haven't shared with my brothers our plan for solving the mystery in the clearing, but I will," Liam told the group.

Their meals finished, the group discussed who would be placed where around the clearing.

"We will all forage for our own food while we are on surveillance," Finn said, taking charge of directing the group, "make our own camps, and make sure they're well hidden. I think we are ready to get started; let's head to the campsite from the other night, and from there, we will split up and go our separate ways around the clearing."

They all gathered their belongings and made their way up the trail towards the bend in the meadow. The three owl brothers took flight, flying on ahead of the group. Reaching the camp faster than the rest of the group gave Liam time to tell Leif and Loki what their roles were in reference to the overall plan.

"I think we should set up our triangle spacing around the clearing, with each one of us in our own territories. That way, when we take turns hunting, we will be familiar with our hunting grounds, and it won't take us as long to get back to observing the clearing. How does that sound to you, brothers?"

They both agreed to his plan. Leif suggested a call for them to use when they wanted to leave their perch and go hunting, and another call for when they returned.

"Brilliant idea," Loki said. "What are we on the lookout for in the clearing?"

"Anything unusual, out of the ordinary; just be careful," Liam warned. "After all, I was hurt by whatever is making the wildlife in the clearing disappear."

"We will be careful," Leif said, "and you do the same."

The rest of their little band of adventurers reached the camp below; Leif motioned with his wing in their direction so the other two owls would see them.

"They are here finally," he said. "I'll drop down and tell Finn our plans, and you two go ahead and fly to your spots, find cover, and sleep. After I share with Finn, I'll find a spot opposite from you and do the same. See you this evening; rest well, brothers."

Liam then dropped down gently to the ground next to Finn and told him their plan. Leaving the other friends to set up their main camp, Liam took off and found a good hiding place, high up in a maple tree across from his two brothers.

After calling to them from his spot so they knew each other's locations, he settled in and was soon fast asleep.

Finn gathered the other friends from around the main camp and said, "We need to start setting up your own campsites around the clearing. Erin and I will use this as our camp, but we will be observing the clearing closer to its edge. We suggest you set your camp up far enough away from the edge so you have protection and observe the clearing; remember to stay hidden at all times. We will all meet back here in two days' time."

The group slowly dispersed, heading off in their assigned directions, each left to decide on where to set up their camps and observation spot for the clearing.

Declan chose the northern point of the clearing, Abby and Asher were going to observe in separate spots but camp together at the northeast point of the clearing, Melody chose the easternmost point of the clearing to do her part of the adventure, and Elijah picked the southern point, it being closer to his village; that way, he could check in with his wife and kids at night, using his home as his camp.

Around midday, the adventurers had reached their assigned areas and began their observations.

Chapter 39

Melody was hopping her way to the farthest spot away from her friend's main camp, deciding to go the northern route, taking her into a part of the woods she had never seen before. As she hopped, she thought to herself, *This is one of those unsettled adventures Finn has talked about so many times,* smiling as she went along. This area of the forest was very different from the part she called home. The ground was hard and dry, and the vegetation was thick and dense, with sharp points and needles, making her travel more difficult. Where she lived, by the stream, she could swim most everywhere she needed to go; here, she had to pick and choose her path very carefully, as not to get pricked or poked as she hopped along.

She soon came across Declan creating his camp; he was using his nose to clear some ground debris in a large circle pattern.

"Hi, friend," she said after clearing her throat and giving a little croak. "Can I help you?"

"Oh, hello, Melody; no, I'm almost done, but thank you," Declan replied. "Abby and Asher just left several minutes ago, heading to where they will make camp, so I'm sure you'll pass them along your journey. Be safe; see you in two days."

"Bye," Melody said, hopping away. "Stay safe; see you soon."

Following the porcupines path made it easier for her to make her way now, and she caught up to her new friends. "Hi, Abby. Hi, Asher," she said as she hopped up next to them.

"Hi, sister Melody. Do you know where you are heading?" Asher asked as she trudged along in front of Abby.

"We are very familiar with this part of the woods and can help if you need it," Abby shared.

"I'll be fine I think, but thank you," Melody replied. "I better get moving; see you both soon."

"See you soon," Asher and Abby said at the same time; they laughed and waved bye to Melody.

The two porcupines continued on for a little while longer, eventually finding a familiar outcropping of conifers.

"This will be good cover," Asher said, "and we won't have to clear the space out for our camp. It's a little farther away from the clearing compared to Declan's camp, but it will be fine."

"Yes, love, it certainly will," Abby replied. "Now that we have our camp site, we better get to our observation spots. I'll go over near the maple tree, and you can take the spot by the mulberry tree; let's meet back here at dusk."

He nuzzled noses with Abby, bidding her farewell. They split up and went to their spots near the clearing to find cover and observe what could be causing the mystery.

After saying bye to Abby and Asher, Melody continued her way through the dense forest. Every once in a while, there would be an opening, making her travel easier. In one of these openings, she noticed scorched burned spots on the ground.

She thought to herself, *I wonder if I'm in the clearing, or is this just where the fire spread from the lightning strike Emmitt told us all about?* Fearing she was in the clearing, she hopped away from the sun's direction eastward, making it back to the thick underbrush, checking her surroundings once she was in hiding again. Deciding she was safe, she continued through the thick vegetation while seeking a great spot to make her camp. The space she found had a large rock in the shape of a flat half-moon sticking up out of the ground, with a uprooted tree laying across it, creating a cave-like opening, great for hiding. Her camp site settled, she hopped back out to find cover near the clearing.

The eastern edge of the clearing had tall trees, some pine, some oak, and a few maples, and lots of ground cover. These would be good for her to use as points of reference as she was on the lookout for whatever it was, over the next two days.

Chapter 40

All their other friends had left to spread out around the clearing except Elijah; he had hung back when the others had departed.

"Finn, I wanted to talk to you before I headed out," he said to the chipmunk.

Erin was busy organizing their camp but heard the mouse's request. "I can go to our hiding spot near the clearing if need be," she said in reply.

"Oh no, sorry, I didn't mean you are to be excluded from our conversation, Erin," Elijah said. "My apologies.

"On one of my excursions from the village, hunting for food, I came across a strange object in the clearing," the mouse said. "This was a few seasons ago, but I'm sure the object is still there. I was afraid to say anything before because of what happened to Liam and Emmitt's consistent warnings about the clearing. I wasn't aware of any danger when I found the object or of the clearing, having not met Emmitt yet, but now I'm afraid to go back there."

When he finished, he looked very concerned that his friends wouldn't understand.

"Well, that's a lot to take in, friend," Finn said, following up with several question: "What does the object look like? How far into the clearing is it located? What time of day was it when you were in the clearing? Do you think you could find it again?"

"Slow down, mister," Erin interjected. "We are not going into the clearing until we have done our work observing for the next two days, plus, our friends are spread out all over, and we have no way of letting them know. Let's be smart and wait the two days to observe the clearing so we can gather information from everyone, before we go traipsing into the clearing."

"This is why I love you so much, sweetheart," Finn said, smiling. "You keep me from getting into serious trouble." He walked over to give her a hug. His arm still around her, he told Elijah, "Better be on your way, and we will see you in two days."

"Okay, but first let me answer your questions," Elijah said. "It was midday when I was in the clearing; yes, I could find it again. I think it is closer to the center of clearing, and it was round and dark, with markings on it. I'll be on my way now; see you in two days."

Elijah headed for his spot near the clearing, leaving Finn and Erin to discuss the information he had just shared.

Elijah was familiar with this area of the woods and reached the trail in no time, then he went to his hiding spot and started observing. Watching the clearing at first, he saw nothing out of the ordinary; listening intently, he heard nothing unusual, either.

Back at the main camp, Erin and Finn made their way to their hidden spot by the clearing and started their watch.

They quietly discussed what Elijah shared with them before he departed. "What Elijah said was very exciting, don't you think?" Finn said. "I can't help but want to run out to the middle of the clearing and find out what he witnessed."

Erin gave him a look of concern and said, "I don't think that would be a good idea, mister; let's be practical about this unsettled adventure. It would be smarter for us to go out into the clearing as a group, once we are all back together. Let's do our jobs observing for the next two days and then go out there."

Finn smiled, nodded, and replied, "This is why you are so good for me; you never let me get ahead of myself, and keep me safe and our friends safe too. That will be our plan, then."

Chapter 41

The rest of the day, the friends hid in their separate spots, observing their parts of the clearing, with no activity to report. They also foraged for their own food, finding enough to last for the next two days. The owl brothers were sleeping in their hiding spots, waiting on the nighttime to begin their observations.

Erin and Finn, about three feet apart in their observation spots, heard a familiar chirp. Ella had found them, having come across Elijah only moments before.

"Well met, friends," she called. "I saw Elijah while flying by his hiding place. Have not been out much because I've been nesting on my eggs; they've hatched now, three little ones to feed, so I'm very busy. Elijah filled me in on what's going on here, and I'll be happy to help when I can, but I'll need to take care of my babies and let my hubby know what I'm doing so he doesn't worry."

"Ella, great to see you," Erin said, excited.

"Congratulations on hatching three little ones," Finn said. "Fantastic news. We are so glad you found Elijah and found us as well. Would you be able to fly around the meadow tomorrow, check in on our other friends, and report back to us? Any help you can give will be greatly appreciated."

"After I feed my babies in the morning," she said, "I'll be happy to visit our friends and come see you again. I need to be getting back to them now; sorry I cannot stay longer. See you tomorrow." With saying that, she took off, not looking back.

As she flew away, Finn said, "She never even told us her babies' names; she must be in a hurry."

"A first-time mother," Erin remarked. "I'm sure she is nervous and always in a hurry."

They watched Ella fly off into the southern sky.

"She must live that direction," Finn said. "Come to think of it, we've never asked her where she calls home. The sun's starting to set, love; we better return to camp and get settled in for the night. I wonder how everyone else is doing around the clearing."

As they started back towards their camp, Erin said, "Guess we will find out tomorrow when Ella comes to visit us again."

Chapter 42

The sun was setting as the two chipmunks reached their little camp; they had a bite to eat and waited for Liam to show up. Not long after they finished eating, Liam landed on a branch just off to the side of their camp.

"How was your day?" he asked. "Anything happen in the clearing?" He stretched his wings out to their full expanse.

"Our day was uneventful," Finn replied. "Nothing to report from the clearing. Have you heard from Leif or Loki yet?"

"Yes, before I left my hiding spot. They are up and ready to keep an eye on the clearing. I better get moving to my spot now."

"Wait a minute, Liam," Erin said. "Finn, you haven't told him about Elijah and Ella."

Finn then shared what transpired with Elijah and about Ella coming to visit and her big news.

"Thanks for letting me know about both things," Liam said. "I'll pass the information along to my brothers, and I'll be off now." Nodding his goodbye to both his friends, the owl took flight.

The night sky was dark, with very few stars showing, as he made his way through the air to his viewing spot high up in the trees. Clouds were coming in on a strong breeze, now covering the clearing. Liam had to hold tight to the branch as it swayed in the hard breeze. The rain started to fall steadily, falling at an angle because of the blowing wind; it was hard for his sharp eyes to see very far into the clearing. *My brothers must be having the same troubles,* he thought to himself. *I will call to them and find out.*

He began to call, "Whoo, whoooot, hoot." He waited and listened; moments passed, and he called again, hearing nothing back from around the clearing except the wind and rain pouring down, striking the leaf-covered trees. He heard the low rolling of thunder from across the clearing. The storm was getting worse now, loud thunder and lightning crashing all around.

Figuring the sounds of the storm deafened his calls to his brothers, Liam decided to hunker down in his viewing spot and ride the storm out. He feared his other friends were not faring so well on the ground surrounding the clearing and hoped his brothers were as safe as he was, for the moment.

Lightning flashed in the sky from time to time, illuminating the clearing. Liam wondered if he might see the object Elijah had described to Finn, but because of the storm's intensity, he wasn't able to see the center of the clearing.

Loud crashes of thunder shook the area, and the soaked tree branches bent and twisted in the wind. Liam could see standing water on the ground now, puddles and small streams flowing downhill towards the south. His viewing spot was in a cluster of branches covered with leaves, but because of the wind gusts, he had moved closer to the trunk of the big maple tree, dropping to lower branches so he wasn't blown out of the tree's thinner branches.

"It's going to be a long night," he said to himself, snuggling closer to the tree trunk. "I hope all my friends are safe as well."

The storm lasted about an hour, with the intense rain and wind, thunder and lightning crashing all around.

After the storm subsided, Liam shook himself dry and stretched. He hopped his way back up to the thinner branches to his viewing spot and called to his brothers; moments later, he heard a familiar call back. It was Loki, and a moment later, Leif's call was heard. All was well; they all made it safely through the storm. Loki's call told them he was going to hunt, and Leif's call shared he's the next to go hunt. Liam's call told his brothers he wanted to check on Finn and Erin first before they hunted. They all agreed, and Liam flew to Finn and Erin's camp, where he found the two chipmunks soaked and tired, being the middle of the night, but doing okay.

"Glad to see you both didn't float away in that terrible storm," Liam said. "My brothers and I are good for the rest of the night. Please try to dry out and get some sleep."

"Thank you for checking in on us," Finn said. "You are a good friend." He reached out his paw to shake Liam's wing.

"Best be off now," Liam said after he let go of Finn's paw and flew back to his viewing spot. The rest of the night was uneventful for the three owls.

Chapter 43

Daybreak found Declan drenched, coming out from under a large inkberry shrub that barely protected him from last night's downpour, the shrub being the closest cover during the storm. The leaves on the ground clung to his muddy, matted fur as he trudged along to his viewing spot. Stopping to eat along the way, he enjoyed a meal of grubs he found under a small rotting log. Upon reaching his viewing spot, Declan shook himself dry and started clearing the mud out of his fur. From time to time, he looked out onto the clearing and wondered if there would be any activity there today.

Asher and Abby climbed down out of the low branches from a leaning conifer tree they used for cover during the storm. Shaking their quill-covered bodies dry, morning found them sleepy from a rough night.

Asher yawned and said, "Morning, love; terrible weather last night."

"Morning, love," Abby replied. "I'm surprised we didn't get washed away from the amount of rain that fell."

They ate some small conifer cones for breakfast. The ground was covered with conifer needles, so there was a barrier between the mud-soaked ground and their paws, making their path to their viewing spots mud-free and easy to traverse.

After they arrived at their separate spots, Asher asked, "All settled in over there, sweetheart?"

"Yes, how about you, love?" Abby replied while using her front right paw to bend a weed out of her sight line of the clearing.

"Yes, I'm ready for anything to happen," Asher replied. "I wonder if Melody enjoyed all the rain we had last night." She leaned into a small bushy shrub for a comfy spot to observe the clearing.

Melody had been concerned about being away from the stream for so long, and she welcomed the storm's rain and moisture soaking the ground. The morning sun's warmth woke her in her resting spot atop a log. She stretched her back legs out one at a time, sunning herself and moving ever so slowly. Opening her eyes, she began searching for her breakfast. Hopping off the log, she soon found insects to eat. Her meal finished, she hopped closer to the clearing and found a nice viewing spot atop a rock with the sun shining directly on it. She thought to herself, *This will do quite nicely for observing the clearing. I wonder how all the rest of my new friends did during the storm last night.*

The morning found Elijah busy with repairs in the mouse village and cleaning up from last night's storm. Giving directions to his family on what needed to be done first and so on, he was in a hurry to be finished with his tasks. "Molly, love, I need to get back to the clearing to start my observations for the day," he said while shouldering his pack. "Will you please take over for me so I can be on my way?"

"Of course, love; with all that was going on here this morning, I almost forgot you needed to go. Don't you worry; we will finish the repairs and cleaning up our village from the storm. Be safe, see you this evening." As he headed up the muddy trail, he turned and called back, "Bye for now; see you this evening, and thank you, love."

He scampered his way up the soggy path, avoiding puddles by leaping over them, landing with a small splash each time. Eventually, Elijah rediscovered his viewing spot and settled in, having to remove some sticks and leaves before relaxing into his day of observation.

Erin rolled gently out of her makeshift hammock and nudged Finn awake, saying, "Wake up, sleepyhead. It's time to get moving."

Finn rolled out of his hammock and replied, "Glad we took the time to make these hammocks last night after the storm. It would have been a wet and soggy time trying to sleep if we hadn't done that."

"You had a really good idea to tie two big leaves together in the middle and attach them on the ends to the sapling elms," Erin said.

"Thank you, but you helped me make them, so kudos to you as well, love. I hope the rest of our little band of friends were alright during the night's storm and were able to get some rest."

Erin handed Finn a berry for breakfast and ate one herself, saying, "This is all the food we have for now until we forage for more later today."

"You could go gather more nuts and berries for us after we visit with Ella," Finn said; he knew Erin would want to be there for their visit with the wren.

"Of course, love," Erin replied. "I'd be happy to. I wonder what time she'll be stopping by?"

The two chipmunks headed back to their viewing spots to watch and wait.

Ella's morning started out busy as usual, making multiple flights out from her nest to gather food for her three newborn babies. Their nest was hidden in a well-established thicket of spruce trees east of the clearing but close to the stream, where the rocks jetted up out of the ground, causing a waterfall, good for protection and sources of food. She had talked to her husband, Kaiden, last evening before the storm came through, telling him she would be gone several hours during the next day and asking if he'd tend to their babies. On her last trip back to their nest, she and Kaiden fed the little ones and discussed their plan for the day.

"Kaiden, I really appreciate you being willing to take care of our little ones while I'm gone," Ella said while rubbing her beak on each one of her babies' beaks goodbye. "I'll try to hurry back from the clearing, but it will take some time. If I'm not home by the evening, please don't worry. I'll be with Finn and Erin at their camp. I promise to be home as soon as I can."

"Please be careful and return safely, sweetheart," Kaiden said in reply while preening Ella's feathers.

Ella rubbed Kaiden's beak, preened his feathers, and said, "See you as soon as I can; take care."

Then she took off for the clearing, flying over the bushes and shrubs, drifting through the trees with ease; eventually, she flew over Elijah's viewing spot. She chirped to him and tilted her right wing, waving as she flew overhead.

Elijah waved and yelled hello to her as she soared above him.

She was flying very fast and didn't say anything in return. Soon, she was flying over Finn and Erin's camp; when she saw the two chipmunks, she landed in between them so they all could talk.

Chapter 44

"Well met, friends," Ella said. "Terrible weather last night; how did you both do during the storm?"

"Well met, Ella," Finn replied. "We made it through alright; how did you and your little ones do during the storm?"

Erin said, "I'm glad you and yours are okay. What are your babies' names? You were in a hurry last night and didn't share their names with us."

"My apologies; I was in a hurry to get back to them. Their names are Killian, the only boy, Eve, and Emma; they were all born within minutes of each other, and hungry right away," Ella shared as she stared out into the clearing.

"Those are beautiful names," Erin said. "Are they growing fast?"

"Oh, yes, they are, and they eat constantly; thanks to Kaiden and myself, they are well fed. What would you like me to find out from our friends around the clearing?" she asked.

Finn told Ella about Elijah's information and asked her to share it with the others and find out if anyone saw anything in the clearing.

"I better get started," Ella said, knowing she had a long way to fly today before she could get back to her babies. "I've got many stops to make but will be back as soon as I can. Bye for now." She lifted off and flew off towards the north part of the clearing.

"Bye, be careful," Erin called. "See you soon."

Finn waved and watched her until he couldn't see her anymore through the trees.

Ella flew swiftly through trees, looking for Declan. The edge of the clearing was a little more open here, with a sparse group of large trees, but the ground cover thick and dense. She found Declan leaning on his back against a large oak tree on the edge of the clearing, his four paws extended out in front of him so the sun could dry his belly and legs. Ella landed silently in the oak tree above Declan, watching him for a moment before chirping to him. Startled, Declan rolled forward on all four paws and shook himself, his black and white thick fur shimmering in the morning's sunlight.

He looked up, cleared his throat, and said, "Hello, Ella; how are you? I'm guessing one of our friends finally found you; are you here on a quest to help us?"

"Oh, yes. I'm here to help. Actually, I found Elijah, and he sent me to find Erin and Finn." She went on to tell him all about Elijah's information and explained Finn and Erin's plan for when they all meet back up the next day. Finishing up, she told him of her good news about her babies.

"Congratulations, Ella," he exclaimed. "That's very exciting. I look forward to meeting them some day."

"Thank you, Declan," she replied. "I'm sure at some point we will all be together, and all our friends will meet them. Lastly, Finn wanted me to ask if you needed anything, and did you see anything in the clearing?"

"I don't need anything," the skunk replied, "and I have nothing to report about the clearing. That storm last night was a doozy, though."

"I will pass along what you said to Finn," she said. "I need to be on my way now; be well and stay safe, Declan. See you tomorrow."

"See you soon," Declan said. "Be safe, and say hi to the others for me." He rose up on his back legs while waving bye with his front paws.

The little wren lifted off from the branch overhead and flew away.

Ella flew off towards the northeast. Her path through the forest was easy at first, coasting after her climb upwards. Eventually, there were more trees, and her flying slowed so she could avoid the trees and leaf-covered branches. She glided effortlessly just above the bushes and shrubs, looking for Asher and Abby. Their brown grayish color was hard to distinguish from the ground cover all around, as Ella swooped through the dense thickets, landing from time to time and calling their names, not sure exactly what they looked like, having never met them before.

The third time, she landed in a small pine tree that was leaning over, resting against another tree. She chirped and whistled, calling the two porcupines' names, "Abby, Asher, are you near my call?"

"Hello there," a voice answered. "Might we ask who is calling our names on this beautiful morning?"

"My name is Ella the wren," she replied. "I'm a good friend of Erin and Finn's. They sent me here to see if you both are okay after the storm and to share some information with you. Will you show yourselves to me?"

"Of course," Asher said. "We will fly around the three trees in front of you, and you will see us."

Ella flew to the right around the three trees and saw two porcupines, one larger than the other. She landed on top of a small maple sapling and said, "Nice to meet you both. I'm Ella."

Asher stepped forward and said, "Well met, Ella. I'm Asher, and this is my wife, Abby. You said something about new information from Finn and Erin. I'm curious as to what that could be."

Ella shared the information with them and then asked if they needed anything; she also told them Declan said hello.

"Interesting," Asher said. "Very interesting; you say Elijah might be able to find this object again? I truly wonder what it could possibly be?"

"As a little bird, my parents warned me about this clearing, so I've always avoided flying through or near it. And I'm a little unsettled flying around it today.

"I best be moving on now," she added. "I'm to fly all the way around the clearing, checking in with all our friends, and then I need to get back to my babies before dark. It was very nice meeting you both; see you tomorrow."

And with that, she took off without looking back, not waiting for their farewells.

The two porcupines looked at each other and shrugged; Abby said, "She must be in a real hurry."

"Agreed," Asher answered and continued watching the clearing.

Turning southeast now, Ella flew faster, hoping to find Melody the bullfrog quickly, as it was now midday, and she still had a long way to go around the clearing. The foliage had mostly dried as she flew, darting in and around trees and shrubs, weaving her way in and out closer to the clearing and back out again. Not sure exactly where Melody will be watching the clearing, she called for her as she flew, having reached the most eastern part of the clearing. Flying close to the clearing, she spotted Melody on a rock right on the edge of the clearing, swooped in, and landed on the rock right next to Melody.

"Hi Melody, I'm Ella," she chirped. "Finn sent me to check in with you."

Melody was a little scared at first but relaxed after hearing her explanation. "Nice to make your acquaintance, Ella. Tell Finn I am doing well. The rain last night was welcomed, and I made good use of the moisture throughout the morning. I've been up here on this rock since the sun rose, staying vigilant watching the clearing."

"I'm glad you are doing well. I'll let Finn know how you are doing. He also wanted me to tell you something Elijah shared with him." Ella went on to share with Melody all about Elijah's discovery.

"Wow, that's sounds incredible," Melody says after Ella finished. "I cannot wait to find out if it's still there."

"I need to be on my way now, Melody. I'll see you tomorrow; bye for now." Ella flapped her wings and lifted off the rock.

"See you tomorrow, my new friend," Melody croaked after her, watching her take off.

Ella flew towards the southwest, where Elijah was waiting and watching the clearing. She knew where he was observing because she had flown over him earlier that morning. Finding him quickly, she landed in a blueberry bush off to his left; after helping herself to a berry or two, she greeted him, "Hi, Elijah; how are you doing?"

"Hello again, Ella; you were flying fast earlier this morning. I'm doing well, just worried about the village. The heavy rains last night created a stream right through the middle of the village, causing a muddy mess and some damage to one of the houses. Molly is overseeing the cleanup and repair while I'm here observing the clearing. My family is helping her take on the cleanup and repairs. How are you?"

"I am doing well, just getting tired from making this trip around the clearing with nothing to report back to Finn. All our friends are okay after the storm and are excited about what you have witnessed in the clearing.

"They all want to go in and find it as soon as possible, that is if it's still there," Ella shared while eating another blueberry.

"I would say you have been flying hard around the clearing," Elijah said. "It's just past midday and you only have to fly back to visit with Finn and Erin. I think you are amazing."

"Thank you," Ella replied. "I'll be going now; I'll see you tomorrow, my friend. Until then, be well." She took off and flew towards Erin and Finn's viewing spot.

"See you tomorrow, Ella," Elijah called after her. "Nice visiting with you again."

Ella flew directly to Finn and Erin's viewing spot and landing in the same spot as earlier. She greeted her friends again.

"Hello again," she chirped. "None of our friends experienced anything unusual around the clearing last night, and they are all doing well after the storm. I shared with them all about what Elijah witnessed, and they all are very interested in looking for what he observed back then. How has your morning been going?"

"Thank you so much, Ella," Erin said. "Our morning has been very relaxed compared to last night's adventure with the storm rolling through."

"We know you need to be flying off home to your little ones soon," Finn said, "but can we offer you something to eat before you go?" He walked over to stand next to Ella and pointed at the spread of berries and nuts Erin had gathered.

"Thank you," the wren said. "I could eat a little more; I had some blueberries while visiting with Elijah before I came here." Ella hopped over to the mound of berries and nuts, helping herself to some berries.

"I'm sure Kaiden will be glad you're coming home earlier than expected, and your babies will be happy to see their mom again," Erin said. "Thanks again for being away from your family and helping us with this unsettled adventure."

"You both are very welcome; after all, solving this mystery will help all of us here in the woods, making it safer for everyone to travel through. I do need to be flying home now; thanks again for the berries, and I'll see you tomorrow."

"See you in the morning," Finn said. "Be safe, and please say thank you to Kaiden for his efforts with the little ones." He walked over to Ella, put his arm around her, and gave her a side hug.

Erin came to her other side and gave her a hug as well.

Ella spread her wings, wrapping them around the chipmunks, and hugged them.

"I'll be off now," Ella said as she lifted gently off the ground between the two chipmunks and flew towards the south, her fastest way home.

She was soon flying over Elijah again; she chirped and fluttered her right wing as a wave towards him. He heard her chirps and shouted his hello as she cruised overhead.

Midafternoon now, flying as fast as she could, Ella made the trip home swiftly, catching insects along the way so she would have a meal to feed her babies once she reached her nest. Having made it home, she was greeted by Kaiden and the three little wrens, all excited and making lots of chirps and coos.

"I'm so glad you're home, honey," Kaiden said while Ella fed their babies. "Any trouble on your quest around the clearing?"

After feeding her little ones, Ella replied, "It all went as well as could be expected. I was able to find everyone pretty easily, and they all were helpful." She told Kaiden in detail about what Finn had said about what Elijah had discovered in the clearing, finishing up with asking him to watch their babies again the next day so she could assist in exploring the clearing with the others.

"That sounds like a very scary endeavor," he said, looking very worried, "and I'm hesitant to agree, but I know how much you have done already, and I could not keep you from seeing this adventure to the end."

"Thank you for understanding, love," Ella said as she rubbed up against Kaiden, showing him her appreciation. They took turns gathering food and feeding their babies for the rest of the day.

Chapter 45

After Ella flew off, Finn and Erin continued their work observing the clearing, and they discussed how they might go about entering the clearing the following day.

"Maybe we should go into the clearing as a group instead of sending our friends in one at a time," Erin suggested.

"I like that idea,"" Finn said. "Safety in numbers; I also think we could have the owls keep an eye on the clearing from the edges while we enter and search for the object. We could have Ella up in the trees as well, keeping an eye out."

"Of course, we'll need to ask everyone if this plan is okay with them," Erin said. "Maybe they have thought of another way to search the clearing."

"Yes, tomorrow, once everyone is gathered back together, we can discuss what is the best plan for all concerned."

The rest of the afternoon was spent in quiet observation of the clearing. The edge of the clearing was visible on both sides of the two chipmunks, each watching with their backs to each other.

"See anything, love?" Finn asked after a long period of silence. "Nothing happening over this direction. I wonder how far it is to the middle of the clearing?"

"That's a good question, dear. I bet one of the owls could tell us because they have a better vantage point up in the trees. I know we can see the trees on the other side, but I'm not sure exactly how far that distance is." Erin stood up on her haunches and looked towards the other side of the clearing.

Finn joined her, rising up as high as he could, trying to see the middle of the clearing.

"You know, we are not very good tree climbers, so I think we should leave the high viewing to our winged friends," he said as he lowered back down on all four paws.

"I knew you were thinking of trying to climb a tree," she said, grinning, "and I'm very glad you are smart enough not to try such a feat."

Soon, the sun started its descent to the west beyond the tree line, the day coming to a close, and the night's adventures ahead. Erin and Finn made their way back to their little camp, far back from the edge of the clearing, and awaited Liam's visit. They ate their dinner and stretched out on the ground next to each other, looking up at twilight's dance beginning; the twinkle of the first stars began to show as the sky darkened. Minutes later, they heard their friend call a greeting of sorts, letting them know he was close by.

Dropping down out of the tall trees, Liam glided effortlessly to the ground right next to them and said, "Hello, friends; how are you today?"

"Hello, Liam; we're fine. Did you sleep well throughout the day?" Erin asked while sitting up to see him better.

"Yes, I did; it was a peaceful day of rest."

Finn shared with him about Ella's helpful trip around the clearing and about their plan for the next day going into the clearing.

"We will need you and your brothers to help," Finn said. "Will you be able to ask them tonight to help us tomorrow?"

"Sounds like a big undertaking," Liam said, "and scary too. Of course, I'll ask them to help. I'm sure you can count on us. I'll be starting my watch now and calling to my brothers. Rest well, friends; see you in the morning."

"Have a safe night, Liam, and thank you," Finn said as he and Erin watched Liam fly up into the tall trees. With nothing more for the two chipmunks to do for now, they crawled into their hammocks and fell fast asleep.

Chapter 46

Liam flew away from his two chipmunk friends to his viewing spot and began to call Leif and Loki. He watched the clearing as he called, but there was no movement besides a constant breeze blowing in from the southwest.

Talking to himself, Liam said, "Hope there isn't another storm blowing in tonight."

The breeze made it hard for him to hear his brothers call back to him, but he eventually made contact with them, finding them both well and willing to help the next morning with the group's adventures into the clearing.

After contacting his brothers, Liam went hunting and then returned to his perch to view the clearing while he ate his catch. Calling out to Leif that it was his turn to go hunt, Liam settled in for the rest of his night's adventure, flying between the different trees, each giving him a different point of view of the clearing. Late in the night, he saw a shimmering movement off towards the east, Loki's area of the clearing. Liam called a warning out to Loki, "WHOOOOT, WHOOOT, WHOOT!" Loki replied quickly he was aware of the movement but was not sure what it was.

He then suggested that Liam fly across the clearing to where he was, and they'd both have a look at the shimmering substance. Liam called back that they should stay put and keep an eye on the shimmering object. He wondered if it might be Spirit, only having seen her from far away; maybe this was her normal look?

Just then, Leif called to Liam, wondering what was going on, having just come back from hunting. Liam told Leif what was happening and asked him if he could see anything from his side of the clearing. Leif responded quickly; he was able to see movement in Loki's direction; it was like the forest was moving, translucent like. This communication continued throughout the night, each owl sharing from time to time what they could see; eventually, the shapeless entity moved towards the center of the clearing and disappeared.

Loki finally went to go hunt shortly before dawn, promising to meet back at Finn and Erin's camp when he was finished.

Chapter 47

Leif and Liam met up in an elm tree just behind Finn and Erin's camp and waited for Loki to join them. Just before the sun peeked its rays above the eastern sky, Loki landed in the elm tree next to Leif.

"Should we fly down and wake up our friends?" Liam asked.

"Yes," Leif said. "I'm sure the chipmunks are ready to get this day started, and hopefully the others are up and coming too so we can find out what that was last night."

All three brothers dropped down out of the elm tree and landed in the camp, where they found Erin and Finn still asleep in their hammocks, so they remained still and rest themselves, having been up all night.

Melody emerged to the morning's chill, having slept under a pile of leaves next to a fallen log. The dawn just underway, she hopped back to where the sun was shining, warmed herself, and began searching for her breakfast of insects, catching them with ease. As she gathered her breakfast, she decided to start hopping her way back to the main camp, thinking to herself, *Maybe I'll meet up with the others along the way.* Following the path she took to get to her viewing spot but in reverse, Melody made good time because she already knew the way.

Soon she was by the leaning conifer tree where she had last saw her porcupine friends.

"Hello, Asher, Abby," she called kind of loud, with a croak at the end.

"Hi, Melody," Asher said, making his way around the three trees to Melody's right. "How was your time watching the clearing?"

Abby followed and said, "Well met; crazy storm night before last. I see you are no worse for the wear."

"And you two as well," Melody replied. "I'm on my way back to the main camp; would you like to join me?"

"That sounds wonderful," Asher said. "Let's go."

And the three started making their way to the north.

The sunshine warmed the trio as they moved through the dense underbrush.

"It's going to be a hot day today," Melody croaked after a long period of silence. "The breaks in the shade are nice."

"Yes, the shade is very nice," Asher agreed, shaking his quills. "We are getting closer to where Declan was camped; keep your senses up. Maybe we will hear him before we see him first."

He was right; they soon heard movement just ahead of them, digging and shuffling sounds.

The three stopped, and Asher cleared his throat and called out, "Declan, is that you making all that noise?"

"Yes, it's me. I'm trying to catch my breakfast; give me a minute." More digging sounds and shuffling was heard, then chewing.

Seconds later, Declan appeared, peeking through a bush. "On your way to Finn and Erin's already?" he asked while stepping forward out of the bush.

"Yes," Melody said. "I guess there wasn't a set time for all of us to meet back up, but I'm excited to discover what is in the clearing, aren't you?"

"Let's be on our way," Abby suggested while taking the lead, walking ahead of the others.

"Sounds good to me," Declan said, falling in line behind Asher, Melody bringing up the rear.

The four made their way towards the main camp near the bend in the meadow.

The nudging from underneath Ella awakened her, and the cries from her babies began as she rose from her nest. Kaiden swooped in and landed next to the nest as she hopped up to an adjoining branch. His throat full of food to feed their three little ones, he began to share between them all. His beak and throat emptied, he said, "Good morning, everyone; did you all sleep well?"

The babies all chirped with excitement, and Ella said, "Yes, I believe we all did. I'll make a few trips out and bring back some food for them and then be on my way to meet up with the group waiting by the clearing."

She then took off and made several trips to and from the nest, each time feeding her three baby birds. Kaiden joined her in her endeavors, each taking turns being with their little ones.

Finally, Ella waited for Kaiden to return; once there, Ella kissed each one of the babies and then kissed Kaiden before saying, "I'll try not to be gone long; thank you for your help, love."

"Always willing to help, sweetheart," Kaiden replied. "Please be safe and return to us as soon as you can."

He wrapped his wings around her, hugging her; she hugged him back, and upon releasing each other, Ella took off.

She flew towards the mouse village, hoping to meet up with Elijah so they could make their journey together to the main camp.

She flew quickly to the west; soon, she was over the dense thickets trail and moments later flying over the mouse village. Slowing her pace, she looked for Elijah but saw Molly first; chirping as she lands, she said, "Hello. Where is Elijah at the moment?"

"He left already for Finn and Erin's camp," Molly shared while smiling at her friend and reaching out her paw to shake Ella's outstretched wing in greeting.

"Oh, okay. I'll try to catch up to him; thank you. See you soon," Ella said as she lifted off the ground, letting go of her paw at the same time.

"Be safe," Molly said. "See you soon; bye for now." She waved to Ella as she flew away.

Not far up the trail, Ella spied Elijah trekking along; she chirped after him, and he turned to see his friend flying towards him.

"Hello, Ella," he said. "Good to see you again this morning."

Ella landed on the ground next to him and said, "Good morning, Elijah. I just left your village after talking with your wife. I could see the village had been repaired; I bet you're glad about that."

The both walked side by side now up the trail towards the main camp.

Their conversation continued as they walk along. Elijah asked how her little ones were doing, and she asked how his were too. Enjoying the morning walk together, they laughed and smiled; soon they were at the trail opening close to the bend in the meadow, not too far off from Finn and Erin's camp.

"I wonder if anyone else is there yet," Ella said, tilting her head to the side.

"Not sure," he replied, shrugging his shoulders. "Time will tell."

The two friends walked on in silence, looking at all the beauty of the surrounding woods.

After circling around a cluster of maple saplings, they reached the camp, where the three owl brothers were sitting on the ground with their eyes closed. Ella flew up into a shrub right above them, and Elijah strolled right past them and unshouldered his pack, resting on it on the ground next to a large tree root. Elijah looked around and saw Finn and Erin sleeping in their hammocks; not wanting to wake any of them up, the two companions sat quietly. Shortly, they heard a yawn, and Finn rolled out of his hammock, stretching his arms and legs at the same time. Erin heard him and crawled out of her hammock, rubbing her eyes and then stretching her arms above her head. Both realized they were being watched at the same time.

Finn yawned again and said, "Hello and good morning."
Not seeing that the owl brothers were asleep as well, his greeting woke them up with a startle.
"Hoot, good morning," Loki said, almost falling over.
Ella dropped down out of the shrub, landing alongside the three brothers, and said, "Good morning to all."
Liam and Leif both nodded their heads, barely able to keep their eyes open, but managed to share a greeting.

Moments later, Abby came walking into the camp, followed by Asher, Declan, and Melody. Welcomes and good mornings shared by all, then Finn climbed up on the large tree root next to Elijah's pack. He cleared his throat and began to tell the friends about the plan for going into the clearing, but then Liam interrupted him.
"Sorry for interrupting you," he said, "but there has been some excitement overnight."
He went on to share with the group what they witnessed overnight; his brothers chimed in with bits and pieces of

information from time to time. Everyone listened intently; all seemed to have questions, but none of them had the answers.

Scratching his head, Finn said, "The only way for us to find out the answers is to go find this thing; any objections to that idea?"

Everyone agreed with the plan and start to gathered themselves for this big, unsettled adventure.

"I know I'm very nervous," Finn said, "and I'm sure the rest of you are too. Let's all stay close to each other in the clearing, and we will be safe. Any sign of trouble, split up and scatter in different directions. Is everyone ready?"

The animals that lived on the ground walked to the edge of the clearing, and the winged friends took to the trees, spreading out in different directions and flying down to the sparse shrubs near their other friends once they saw the clearing was safe.

The three owl brothers and Ella had been directed by Finn to fly on ahead of the group but stay spread out to give the others a bigger path to follow. Finn and the rest of the group moved out into the clearing; they huddled together as they made their way through the short foliage. Declan and the two porcupines were larger than some of the ground cover and could see ahead of the others and give directions.

The feathered friends chirped, whistled, and hooted that the way was safe, staying in constant communication with everyone. Liam led the way; closing in on the center of the clearing, he lifted off the ground about a foot and a half to get a better idea of how much farther the group needed to go.

Flying back down, he called out to Finn, "There's something just ahead of us; it's hard to see because it's covered up by weeds and tiny shrubs, but I can see something shining through the foliage."

The group moved slowly forward, and the winged friends joined them. Liam walked in front alongside of Finn, pointing his wing in the direction they needed to go. Finally, the whole group reached the object; Finn and Declan removed the weeds out of the way by pulling them out of the ground, while Asher and Abby pushed the tiny shrubs to the side.

Elijah stepped forward and said, "This is what I saw a long time ago."

He reached his paw out and touched the object; it looked like a rock made of metal. Strange markings covered the shiny object, some etched inward and others protruding outward.

"It feels solid," Elijah said. "And it's hot to the touch. I thought it would be cold."

All the others took turns touching the object; a few moved around to the other side and looked at the markings. Erin found two round markings on the backside of the object one smaller than the other. They looked like buttons and did not seem like any of the other markings, which were lines and swirling shapes, some touching others and some not.

Excited, Erin cried, "Look at these shapes; they're different than the rest."

The rest of the group took turns looking, but no one touched the buttons, having already touched the other markings.

"That's very strange," Melody said. "I'm not sure if we should keep on touching this thing."

Abby, Ella, and Erin followed her example and took a step backwards away from the object, leaving only the males near the strange rock.

"I think it's become hotter since we started touching it," Leif said, tracing one of the markings with his wing.

"I think you're right," Loki said, taking his wing away from where he was also tracing a marking.

"Let's all move back away from it and see if there are any matching markings," Finn suggested.

The group of friends formed a circle around the object; standing about half a foot away, they began to search. The metal-looking gray rock, about three feet around, was almost buried in the ground; it began to make a low-pitched vibrating sound, like metal rubbing metal.

"Look at the markings," Elijah yelled. "Do you see? They are moving."

"The round markings are not moving at all," Erin said.

They all moved around to where Erin was standing; all the other markings were slowly moving, the vibrating sounds still low. Ella lifted off the ground and flew directly over the rock, landing a few feet away on the other side.

"I think we should move far away from it now," she said loudly.

"Why?" Finn asked. "What did you see when you flew over the top?"

"Nothing, really," she responded nervously. "I just think for safety's sake, we should get out of here in a hurry."

"Let's all move back," Erin said, "about ten paces away." She put her arms out to gently push her friends on either side back.

Melody hopped clear over the object, landing right next to Ella and almost colliding into her. "Sorry, Ella," she croaked. "I'm with you. I'm scared; let's go."

Late morning, the sun was almost at its apex when the group of friends backed away from the object and gathered together.

"Do you think we are far enough away?" Liam asked, directing his question to the whole group.

"Let's back up some more," Leif suggested, nudging Loki to move farther away from the object.

The others followed and ended up being about twenty paces away when they finally stopped.

"I know we are all scared," Finn said. "Let's take a break and settle down."

Some of the friends sat down on the ground; Loki and Leif took refuge in a small shrub. Asher put himself between the object and his friends, turning sideways to block them from its view. Abby noticed what he did and joined him, standing nose to nose with him.

Liam saw what they were doing and said, "Thank you two; that's very kind of you," pointing in their direction so the others could see what they had done.

"You're welcome," Asher said. "Our quills can protect us if anything was to come out of that thing."

Finn walked closer to them and leaned in to listen. "It's still making that sound," he said, turning his head so he could look over at Asher. "It has stopped moving now; wonder what that means?"

"I'm sure we don't know." Erin replied, looking at the others for confirmation.

Ella and Melody, the farthest away, nodded their heads; Liam had flown up to join his brothers.

"Beats me," Asher said, sitting right next to Finn. "Your guess is as good as mine."

"Can you owls see it from up there?" Finn asked.

"Yes," Leif said. "The markings are not moving now."

"Shush, shhh, quiet now," Abby announced, holding a paw up to her mouth.

They all stopped moving and talking. The low-pitched vibration was gone.

Finn scratched his head and said, "Stranger and stranger."

Declan cleared his throat, paused for a moment, and then said, "I think we should wait it out right here; the owls said it was active last night, so maybe it only really shows what it is in the dark."

"Wait, wait, wait a minute," Ella said. "We don't even know if what they saw is the same thing we are seeing right now. Anyways, I cannot be gone over night. I need to fly home and take care of my babies."

"Ella, no one is suggesting that you stay," Finn replied. "If anyone wants to leave, it's okay; everyone is free to leave at any time. I do think Declan's idea is a good one; we should take a vote. All those in favor, raise a paw or wing or flipper."

Looking at his friends, Finn counted seven raised appendages; all the males voted to stay put. "Okay, I take it that the ladies want to exit the clearing for safety reasons, and that's fine. We will stay here and see what happens, and then we'll meet you at the camp in the morning. Is that okay with everyone?"

They all nodded their heads yes, and the ladies prepared to leave.

"What about food, love?" Erin asked. "Is there anything else you might need?"

"We can follow you all out of the clearing, gather what we need, and come back here to make camp for the night." Finn looked at his friends for agreement.

They all nodded.

"I'll be flying home once we reach the edge again," Ella said. "This is very exciting, and I want all of you to be safe."

The little band of adventurers made their way back to the main camp.

Staying together as they moved, the owl brothers flew from small shrub to small shrub; Ella joined them, Asher and Abby bringing up the rear of the group. They zigged and zagged through the sparse ground cover, eventually making it back to where they entered the clearing.

Ella bid them all good luck and farewell, adding, "I'll come back tomorrow morning."

She took off and didn't look back, flying away fast as she could. In turn, each friend said goodbye before she took flight, leaving them to face the unsettled feelings about what was going to take place over the next several hours.

Chapter 48

Finn and the others ate a meal of berries and nuts; Declan and Melody went out in search of insects and came back after eating their fill. The owls said they would wait and eat later that night.

"I think it would be prudent if one of you owl brothers stayed with Melody, Erin, and Abby here near the edge," Finn said. "That way, you could fly into the clearing and bring back information to our loved ones. Any volunteers?"

Loki said, "I'll stay and watch out for them. How will I know to fly in and check on you all?"

Finn scratched his head and said, "Good question. I guess come check on us when you want to, maybe once or twice before nightfall, and then to relieve your brothers when they need to go hunt."

"Sounds good," Loki replied.

"Thank you for volunteering," Finn said. "Let's go back into the clearing."

Motioning for the rest of his friends to follow him, Finn gave Erin a hug and then departed for the clearing. Declan, Asher, Liam, and Leif followed him. This time more confident in their travels, they made their way back easily. They set up a makeshift camp, the object about ten feet away in full view. They discussed taking shifts watching the object and searching for easy exits, if needed, from the clearing.

All that being figured out, the small group settled in for the long haul. First to move closer to the object was Declan, taking the first observation shift. Creeping about two feet away, Declan called back to the others, "It's still not making any noise, and the markings haven't moved."

"Don't go any closer," Finn said. "Just keep an eye on it, and let us know if anything changes."

Asher crawled under a small shrub and said, "I'm going to rest for a bit. I have the first shift after dark, so I want to be wide awake for that."

He chuckled as he shut his eyes. Elijah did the same as Declan, finding a shady spot to sleep and saying, "I need a little rest myself. Hope that's okay with everyone."

The others all nodded in agreement.

Leif and Liam were sitting on the ground next to Finn. Liam said, "Wonder if what we saw last night is inside that thing. Is that where it sleeps during the day? Are the sound it's making and its markings a warning of some sort, like protection for it?"

"That would make a lot of sense," Leif replied, "but I think we will just have to wait and see."

The rest of the afternoon was uneventful; none of them moved any closer to the object. Loki came to visit for a little while, reporting that their loved ones at the main camp were doing well, then he flew back to share with the others what was happening in the clearing. The evening began with the sun starting its climb downward behind the forest's treetops.

The six friends were all on alert and awake now; they took up positions surrounding the object, standing closer but not close enough to touch it. They were waiting on Loki to arrive, and soon Loki flew in and landed between his brothers, making the circle complete.

"Well met, friends," he said. "The ladies are all settled in for the night but are worried about what's going to happen out here. What's the plan?"

Finn began to talk about what he hoped would happen that night. The object looked dull and gray in the pale evening moonlight, the sky not quite dark enough to lend to the moon's brightness.

Still no sound could be heard or movement of the markings as the seven friends surrounded the object.

"Let's take a few steps closer and see what happens," Elijah suggested as he stepped closer.

The others followed his lead and approached the object. As they edged closer, the low sound began again, along with the markings moving again. They all paused, standing still and waiting, all ready to run, fly, or hide. Just then, a smoky vapor appeared from the button markings. The smaller button collapsed into the larger one, releasing the smoky vapor. They all fell backwards on their backsides, looking upwards as the aberration grew larger above them. Staggering, they backed up as a group a few paces, widening their circle. The swirling vapor circled closer to the group, making a few passes around in front of them.

The shimmering vapor slowed and stopped at Elijah, completely surrounding him; translucent, the others could see him and the entity combining with each other.

In Elijah's voice but deeper, the entity spoke: "Curious, strange." He cleared his throat. "This is the only way I can communicate with you animals; that is what you are called, right? Not to fear; your companion will not be harmed. I have traveled from far beyond your limited understanding; well, maybe not. I am what you would call a star, or what's left of one. I have existed for a very long time. I recall a beginning, a black void, and then feeling others, then after some time a brilliant light; after that, I could see what I had felt for a long time before, the others like me, moving through the darkness. Sometimes they would collide, exploding apart, crashing through the light and darkness. Eventually, this happened to me, sending me on a collision course with this place. Traveling here took longer than I had existed prior to the collision. As I traveled across the darkness, I grew smaller and smaller, passing by other stars and larger brighter stars, finally colliding with this big star."

When he finished its tale, the group of friends were in shock.

After some moments, Finn managed to ask, "Do you want to be left alone?"

"I am used to lots and lots of space, so to answer your question, yes, but I am confined to this area." He used Elijah's body to turn around in a circle, pointing as he turned him around. The entity pointed at the tree-lined clearing and explained, "I am now a star wraith; I'm only able to be that far away from my home without disappearing completely."

"Now that we have met you and know a little more about you and what your wishes are, we will stay out of your clearing," Liam announced, stepping away from Elijah.

"I would like that, and in return, I will not harm any of you again. In time, I will fade away completely, each passing rotation around that big bright star causes my energies to diminish." He used Elijah's finger to point to the west, where the sun had set not long ago. "When I am no longer a wraith, this clearing will have all new growth and new life to live in and on it, but until that time, I wish to be left alone."

Shimmering and shaking, Elijah's body fell to the ground, and the star wraith rose out of his body, swirling in the night sky above the small group. Elijah rose to a sitting position, elbows on his bent knees, hands on his head, and said, "Goodness, that was something."

The others helped him up. Finn slipped an arm under his shoulder to hold him up. Clearly shaken by the experience, Elijah needed help to walk.

"We will be on our way now," Declan said. "We are all glad to meet you, and we will pass along your wishes to be left alone and to stay out of the clearing."

He and Asher moved around the grounded star, the others already moving in a line towards the main camp.

The owl brothers stayed on the ground, afraid to fly away; they followed behind Finn, helping Elijah make his way along. The star wraith swirled just above them the whole way to the edge of the clearing. The main camp was a little way from the edge of the clearing; the star wraith departed once the little band passed through the dense underbrush.

The group reached the main camp, receiving greetings from the three waiting friends. Excitedly, Erin greeted Finn and showered him with hugs and kisses. She then turned her attention towards Elijah, visibly shaken from his experience.

"What happened, Elijah? Are you okay?" she asked.

Abby had waited for Asher to step through the underbrush and greeted him by rubbing noses. Melody did a head count as the group came into camp, and she said, "All present and accounted for; seems like you're the only one worse for the journey, Elijah. Tell us what happened."

Liam said, "Not true; we are all shaken up. He's just the one that had his body possessed."

Erin stepped closer to Elijah and offered him a drink as she looked him over closely. Rubbing her head with her paw, she said, "Have you always had that white patch of fur?"

All the others leaned in and looked at their friend.

"White fur?" Elijah said. "I've always been tannish brown all over."

The white patch of fur was located behind his left ear; it was circular, with three points coming out of it opposite of each other, kind of like a triangle under the circle. Finn described its shape to Elijah and then shared what happened in the clearing. The three females listened intently, and the other friends helped with sharing, describing in detail what they experienced in the clearing.

"We couldn't see or hear anything that was going on in the clearing," Erin said, motioning to Melody and Abby for them to agree, and they nodded their heads.

"I don't recall anything that happened after the vapors were coming out of the star on the ground," Elijah said, still touching behind his left ear, trying to feel if he could tell the difference in his fur there.

"That is probably a good thing, friend," Finn said, walking over and putting a paw on his shoulder. "Are you sure you are feeling alright after that experience?"

"Yes, I don't feel any different," Elijah said.

"Good," the rest of the group replied, all showing their concern.

It was late, maybe the middle of the night now; the owl brothers said they were going to go hunting and would return at sunrise. After checking on Elijah, they took off without saying anymore to the group. The camp was silent for several minutes.

Finn broke the quiet by inviting the rest of the group to stay overnight in their camp. "It would be nice if we all shared breakfast in the morning before going our separate ways," he said.

The others agreed to stay overnight. Asher and Abby found a low-hanging conifer tree close to the edge of the clearing and disappeared underneath its branches. Elijah curled up next to the large tree root and fell asleep without a word. Declan ambled over to the underbrush and slipped in underneath, his black-and-white bushy tail still visible. Melody hopped over Elijah and found her resting spot between two large roots closer to the trunk of the big walnut tree. Erin and Finn crawled into their hammocks. Soon, all were asleep.

Chapter 49

Morning greeted the group with the warm sunrays shining down on them. Waking up later than usual, Finn could hear Elijah and Melody conversing. Nudging Erin's hammock, Finn gently woke her up, saying, "Love, our friends are already awake, and we need to start gathering food for breakfast."

Erin crawled out of her hammock, stretched, and said, "Good morning, sweetheart. I'll go out right away and find some food for us all."

Melody spoke up and said she would help as well, and they departed from the camp.

Declan soon rolled out from under the ground cover and greeted his friends. Abby was the first to emerge from low branches of the conifer tree; Asher appeared moments later, and both shook their quills to realign them from the night's rest. When Erin and Melody returned, they laid out the berries and nuts; Erin brought out her little pack and shared the last of their biscuits. Everyone helped themselves to the spread before them.

Ella swooped in, landing on the ground behind everyone; she chirped a greeting to everyone.

"Good morning," she said. "Is everything good here? What happened last night? Where are the owl brothers?"

Finn stopped eating and said, "Come to think of it, I fully expected them to be here at daybreak, like they said. I hope they are alright."

He then went on to tell Ella about the wraith, and Elijah told his part of the adventure. They finished sharing, and Finn suggested that the group call out for the owl brothers. Everyone agreed, and they began to shout their names, pausing to listen in between shouting. Finally, Liam flew into the camp.

"Good morning, good morning," he said. "Sorry for being late; after hunting last night, my brothers decided to go back to their own territories; they asked me to extend their farewells and said they will come visit soon. Then I fell asleep until I heard you all shouting for me."

Everyone enjoyed their meal and talked about the plans for the day ahead. After a while, Finn climbed up on the large root and began, "This has been a crazy few days and nights, and we want to thank you all for your efforts and sacrifices."

Erin joined him, standing on the root, and added, "We need to spread the word to our families and other woodland friends about the clearing and the wraith that dwells there."

"Let's plan to gather together again in a month's time at our home in the meadow," Finn suggested. "How does that sound to everyone?"

They all agreed and started their goodbyes, taking their time visiting with one another.

Declan headed out first, followed by the two porcupines, Asher and Abby; Elijah, Ella, and Melody decided to travel together back to the mouse village, and then Ella and Melody would continue on to their homes alone. They said bye to Finn, Erin, and Liam and headed towards the trail opening; soon, they were out of sight.

The two chipmunks started to clean their camp and pack things up for their trek home.

Liam assisted them while expressing his gratitude to them, saying, "I would not be alive if it weren't for your caring ways and desire to help me. I hope to return your kindness someday." He walked over and hugged them both, one at a time.

"I will see you in the meadow from time to time," Finn said, "and definitely will be at your home in a month. Farewell until the next time we meet."

"It was an amazing, unsettled adventure," Erin added, "and it was our pleasure to help you heal. We are so glad you are all better. Please feel free to come by and visit us anytime. Farewell, our friend."

Liam turned away from them and took flight up into the trees, disappearing from their view.

The two chipmunks followed his flight until they could no longer see him, then they turned, faced each other, and then hugger.

"Let's go home," Finn said, while releasing her from their hug.

"Yes, let's go home," she replied. "It seems like we have been gone for a long time."

They shouldered their packs and set off for home.

Chapter 50

Walking side by side, holding paws as they hike homeward, Finn and Erin enjoyed the morning's fresh air; soon they reached the bend that opens to their meadow. The morning sun was shining through in breaks from the trees, like streams, warming them as they made their way home.

"Almost home, love," Finn said. "It will be nice to get back to our regular routine."

"Yes, that will be nice," Erin replied. "Ah there it is: home."

The colorful wildflowers made them happy to see their beautiful spot in the world. Everything was as they left it days earlier; the big table still had the centerpieces on top, but they looked old and decaying. A few leaves had fallen to the ground, some leaning on the table and chairs that needed to be cleared away, but other than that, their home was as they had left it.

Finn went inside to check that everything was safe; he came back out and said, "Good to be home; all clear inside."

Erin scampered inside, taking both their packs with her, saying, "After I unpack these, I'll come back and help you clean up out here."

"Sounds good," he replied. "I'll get started."

He started gathering the leaves and carrying them away out into the woods; Erin soon joined him, and they took the centerpieces from the table and carried them out past the tree line, away from their home in the meadow. The seeds from the now-dead flowers would be scattered and grow new beautiful flowers for them and others to enjoy.

Their work cleaning up finished, the two chipmunks climbed up the root ball on the back of their house to the top of the log.

They sat down and looked out over their surroundings; Finn said, "Love, I'm so glad we are on this unsettled adventure of life together." He leaned in and kissed her cheek.

"Every day with you is a good adventure, love," Erin replied, grinning and blushing.

"I wonder if Emmitt ever met the star wraith," he said. "What would he think of our unsettled adventure in meeting the entity?"

The sun's shadows in the meadow grew larger as the sun began to set. Erin reached over, took Finn's paw, and said, "I'm sure Emmitt knows what has transpired over the last few days and is happy we are all home safe now."

"I agree. I cannot help but wonder what our next unsettled adventure will be?" Finn replied, smiling that grin Erin knew all too well.

Printed in the United States
by Baker & Taylor Publisher Services